IVFOL

Seven Daughters & Seven Sons

I slipped out of the gate, hoping I had at least an hour until first light. I strode swiftly through the narrow, winding streets. Occasionally, a dog barked at me. I passed a woodcutter carrying a load of sticks on his back and a farmer leading a donkey loaded with palm rib boxes full of chickens. A dairyman with two pails yoked over his shoulders jostled me as I went by. It was still dark, but already buyers and sellers from outlying villages had begun to trade. No one gave me a second glance. My disguise was working. I was just a boy and, like everyone else, merely on my way through the dusty, crooked streets of the Suq al-Thalatha, the Tuesday market, the oldest and longest bazaar on the Rasafa, the eastern side of the Tigris River.

Seven Daughters & Seven Sons

by Barbara Cohen and
Bahija Lovejoy

A BEECH TREE PAPERBACK BOOK • NEW YORK

First edition published in 1982 by Atheneum.
First Beech Tree Edition, 1994.
Printed in the United States of America
9 10

Library of Congress Cataloging in Publication Data
Cohen, Barbara
Seven daughters and seven sons / by Barbara Cohen and Bahija Lovejoy.
p.   cm.
Summary: A retelling of a traditional Arabic tale in which a
young woman disguises herself as a man and opens up a shop in
a distant city in order to help her impoverished family.
ISBN 0-688-13563-3
[1. Folklore, Arab.]   I. Lovejoy, Bahija Taffuhi.   II Title.
III. Title: Seven daughters and seven sons.
PZ8.1.C6644Se   1993
398.21–dc20   94-80   CIP   AC

Part 1

THESE ARE THE WORDS written long ago by Buran, daughter of Malik, a poor shopkeeper of Baghdad. She put them down so that her children, and their children, and their children, and all those who came after them would know of the remarkable events that had given rise to their illustrious line.

And wonder of wonders, she wrote all these words in her own hand, forming each beautiful Arabic letter with perfect precision and grace, for her father had taught her to read and write when she was very young, even though it was not the custom in her time for girls to learn such things. Read these words, then, and open your eyes wide in amazement at the marvels that Allah has wrought.

1

I AM BURAN, daughter of Malik, and the fourth of the seven female children born to him, and to his wife of holy memory, my mother, Zubaydah. My father was called Abu al-Banat, the father of daughters, and the title was not considered an honorable one. Allah had not seen fit to bless him with sons, and all that happened afterwards stemmed from that fact. O my children, the ways of Allah are beyond human understanding. What we imagine to be a blessing can actually be a curse, and what we suppose to be a curse may blossom into a blessing.

The marvelous chain of events about which I will tell you began one evening as I sat in the courtyard with my father, playing chess.

It was spring. The scent of jasmine hung thick in the air. As we moved first one piece and then another, the pale light died away. The moon had not yet risen. The wooden shutters on the windows of our little house

3

of baked bricks had been removed, and the light from the oil lamps inside made bright squares on the ground. But our board was too far from the windows to catch the light, and in time it grew too dark to see the chessmen.

With his hand, my father swept the pieces aside. "That's enough of that," he said. "O my daughter, I declare you the winner."

"But Father," I assured him, "I wasn't even close to putting your king in check."

My father laughed. "Six moves more, seven moves more, what difference does it make? Sooner or later you would have checked my king, and mated my king, just as you always do. It was a dark day for me when I taught you this foolish game. Your mother scolded me. She said your time would be better spent with your needle or your loom than in learning men's amusements." He sighed, a vast mock sigh. "Ah me. I should have listened to your mother."

"O my father," I murmured, "I'm glad you didn't." I knew he was glad too. He loved to play chess; it was a precious distraction from his daily struggle to support our crowded household. Since he had no sons, he had been forced to teach the game to one of his daughters, if he was to play it at all, for he had neither the time nor the money to gamble with other men in the shops of the suqs. I, Buran, was the one he had chosen. Perhaps he chose me because I was so clumsy at all the tasks my mother set me around the house that

4

he felt it was I she could best spare. Or perhaps he chose me because I was the one who wanted with all my heart to learn.

I knelt on the ground to pick up the scattered pieces. In the street beyond our wall I could hear voices and the sound of footsteps echoing in the night. The footsteps halted at our gate, and through the wooden slats I caught a glimpse of lantern light and the whirl of two or three striped jubbas fashioned of fine linen. Even before my father spoke, I knew who had stopped at our house.

"Go indoors," my father ordered. "Tell your mother to prepare a drink of yogurt. Your uncle and some of his sons have come to call on me," he added with a sigh. It was a real sigh this time.

Our house was small. It was necessary for my father to detain my uncle and cousins in our courtyard while my mother prepared the drink and laid out a few sweetmeats. "A paltry display," she complained, "but it's the best I can do. It's all we have." I knew that was true. "Your uncle is unbelievably thoughtless to call on his brother here at home," my mother continued crossly. "He knows we can't afford to entertain him properly. Why didn't he go to see your father in the shop, the way he usually does?"

When the food was laid out, she, my sisters, and I withdrew to the other room. My sisters were soon busy with their sewing and their embroidering, their spinning and their gossiping, though what they found to

5

talk about so endlessly when they went nowhere and saw no one was beyond my comprehension. Still, I envied them, for they never seemed to be afflicted with the fits of melancholy that overcame me when I wondered what would become of them, what would become of me, what would become of all of us. "Allah will provide," they always said. "Allah will provide." And then they would go on with their ceaseless stitching, their endless chatter. They were content to be just what they were. There were times when I longed to jump right out of my skin and into someone else's, like my cousin Hassan's, or my cousin Ali's. It was they who had come to call on my father, along with my uncle.

I stood by the curtained doorway and listened to the conversation between my father, his brother, and my two oldest cousins. It was wrong to listen, but I'd always done it; and so accustomed were my mother and my sisters to this habit of mine, that they'd long ago stopped scolding me for it. I think they were rather glad I listened because then I could tell them all that had been said. That is, I told my sisters. My father told my mother.

"Your visit does honor to my poor home," I heard my father intone politely as he escorted his brother and his nephews out of the courtyard, through the arched hall or iwan, and into the main room of the house.

"Well, there's a reason for it, O father of girls,"

my uncle said. His proud, sneering voice always made me want to shake him. How could my father be so unfailingly polite to him, so pleasant? It wasn't because my father, a poor man, expected any help from his brother, though my uncle could have provided bridal gifts for all seven of us and never even noticed that the money was gone. Generous, courteous, and kind, my father's manner was the same whether he was talking to a beggar or to the richest merchant in Baghdad. But my uncle didn't know that. He was accustomed to receiving the grossest flattery, simply because he was rich. Most people he encountered perhaps thought they could get something from him. My father knew better.

"O my brother, please seat yourself, please drink some yogurt before you tell me why you've honored me this evening," my father urged. Just "O my brother," not "O father of sons," or even "Abu Hassan." This was the only expression of annoyance that my father permitted himself, and I'm sure my uncle didn't even notice. He wasn't in the habit of really listening to anyone he regarded as less important than himself.

I moved closer to the curtain and pushed it aside so that the merest crack of space appeared between the curtain and the jamb. Now I could see into the room. I could see my father and my uncle and my two cousins sitting on cushions and sipping yogurt from copper cups. My father didn't touch the sweets, and my uncle only nibbled at them to be polite, but Hassan and Ali gobbled up every morsel on the plate, oblivious to the fact that on account of their greed, their seven cousins would have nothing but beans and onions to eat for the rest of the week.

"Listen to me, O father of girls," said my uncle. "Your eldest nephew, Hassan, knows his duty to the members of his family. He's come to take his leave of you. At first light tomorrow, he departs with the caravan for the coast, and from there he sails to Alexandria."

"Alexandria!" my father cried. "Alexandria! So far away! Why do you go, O my nephew?"

I wanted to cry out too. Of my uncle's seven sons, I loved my cousin Hassan the best, even if he was a greedy young man who'd just eaten up all of our cakes. When I was little, he hadn't been like his brothers. He'd been willing to play hide and seek and tag in the courtyard with me, even though I was a girl. Of course, as we got older we weren't allowed to see each other face to face, but nevertheless, I had managed to catch glimpses of him through windows and curtains, just as I was doing now. He had grown into a handsome man, with soft dark eyes, curling black hair, and a wide, smiling mouth. I focused every scrap of my attention on him as he answered my father. "Uncle," Hassan said, "I'm going to Alexandria because my father wants me to go. He's given me enough capital to set up shop there. Think of the advantages to him of having both an outlet and a source in two cities, instead of in Baghdad alone."

"As soon as Hassan's on his feet, I'm to leave," Ali announced proudly. "I'm to set up on the island of Cyprus."

"It's a wonderful thing to have sons," my uncle said. "Allah has blessed me beyond belief. Seven sons. Seven healthy, intelligent sons. It's something you can't imagine, O father of daughters."

"My daughters are beautiful girls, modest girls," my father replied quietly. "Each one is more precious to me than all the jewels in the caliph's vaults."

"Of course, of course," my uncle replied in a tone heavy with condescension. "Naturally you love them. They're good girls, very good girls. But after all, of what use are so many of them?" He smiled and sipped his yogurt. My poor father didn't answer. What answer could he make? All of Baghdad considered him, with his seven daughters, as cursed as his brother of the seven sons was blessed. The fact that he was poor and his brother was rich only served to reinforce the general opinion.

"And listen to this, my uncle," Ali went on. "When I'm properly established in Cyprus, my brother Ibrahim will set up shop in Sidon. And when he's established, the next one will go, and the next, and the next, and the next. Soon there won't be an important town on the eastern end of the Mediterranean Sea that doesn't boast a branch of Abu Hassan, Merchant Suppliers. We'll corner all the goods, and in no time, we'll have cornered all the money too!"

"You'd better leave a little bit for your customers," my father commented, the faintest touch of asperity in his voice. "Otherwise, how will they manage to buy from you?"

"Not to worry, uncle," Hassan said, his black eyes gleaming in the lamplight. "The sons of my father will spend as well as earn. We won't live like beggars in the cities where we set up shop. We'll live as befits our station."

"As befits your station," my uncle interrupted severely. "No better."

"And no worse," Hassan replied, still smiling. I smiled too, behind the curtain. Hassan hadn't changed in all these years. Perhaps he was now a man of business, but still the most important thing in life to him was having a good time.

My father reached out and touched his brother's hand. "O son of my mother," he said, his forehead wrinkled, his voice slow, as if he found what he now had to say difficult to get out of his mouth, "listen to me. Wouldn't it be wise to see that Hassan is properly married before you send him off to a strange city, where he'll be exposed to all kinds of temptations, far from strong and loving hands to guide him?"

My uncle's eyes were narrow, though his lips

smiled. "I daresay you have a suitable wife in mind, O father of daughters," he replied, his voice cold.

My father bowed his head. "My Buran," he said. I could scarcely hear him, his voice was so low. But my heart leaped at his words. It was my second most cherished dream to be the bride of my cousin Hassan. My first most cherished dream was so fantastic that I hardly ever dared to dream it. And perhaps if my second one came true, I'd be willing to give up the first one entirely.

"Your Buran?" Hassan echoed. "Your Buran?" I watched him shake his head vigorously.

My father didn't see that gesture. "Why not?" he asked, lifting his own head and speaking more firmly now. "Her mother named her for Queen Buran, whose wedding two hundred years ago was so lavish that it remains to this day a byword for magnificence." His smile was wry. "I can't provide my Buran with any but the simplest wedding. You know that as well as I. But what of that? What's important is that my Buran, like her namesake, is as clever as she is beautiful. Besides, she's your cousin. What could be more suitable?"

"O my brother, believe me," my uncle said, his voice thick with oily politeness, "if she came to her husband with just a little something, just the barest smidgen, beyond her own lovely self, I wouldn't hesitate a moment. I think, though, that it would be more appropriate for you to offer Fatimah, your eldest, who to my mind is certainly the best looking." Then he shrugged. "But what difference does it make? Hassan won't marry any of them, and neither will any of my other sons." The courtesy had slipped out of his voice, and its usual harshness filled the room. "It's not for them to marry girls from poor families. They'll marry the richest girls I can find for them."

"My Buran will be a true helpmeet to the man fortunate enough to win her," my father replied proudly. I was filled with joy at his words. I had always known that he loved me, but until that night, I hadn't known how much. "Her eyelash is worth more than all the gold of the wealthiest girl on earth."

"Come now, brother," my uncle said. "You never were a practical man, never. That's why you're no further along in business today than you were when you started out. May Allah bless you and all of your daughters. May he send them husbands worthy of their beauty and their goodness. But those husbands won't be sons of mine. I don't like to imagine whose sons they will be," he added unnecessarily, "since you can provide them with nothing."

My father turned toward Hassan. For all my joy at discovering how much I meant to my father, it hurt my heart to see him forced to humble himself for our sakes. "Hassan, you were fond of Buran when you were a boy. It was always the dearest wish of my heart that one day you two would make a match of it."

Hassan laughed. This time the sound didn't ring as pleasantly in my ears as it had a moment before. "Oh, she was just a tagalong," he said lightly. "She insisted on playing boys' games. What was I to do? Beat her off? Now I don't even know what she looks like. Why should I be saddled with a girl who's poor and probably ugly to boot? Uncle, you mustn't presume on our relationship."

How dared Hassan speak so to my father? How dared he speak to him without respect? But his own father said nothing. His own father didn't scold him for such inexcusable rudeness. My uncle didn't even correct Hassan when he called me ugly, and my uncle certainly knew better. I was the least beautiful among the seven of us, but to be least in such a company could scarcely be catalogued as ugly.

My father rose from his seat. "Listen to me, Hassan," he said. "You're a free man. You can refuse to marry anyone, including my daughter. But you dare not speak ill of her before her own father. I think it would be wisest if you left now."

"Brother, you're too hasty—" my uncle began.

"May your journey be a safe one, Hassan." My father ignored his brother. "May Allah prosper you in all you undertake. May he keep you in health. And may he save you from regretting the things that you have said in this house tonight!" Without another word, he turned his back on them, crossed the floor,

13

and passed through the curtain into the room where I was waiting with my mother and my sisters.

He stopped short when he saw me standing at the opening. He knew I'd been eavesdropping. "I'm sorry you heard what you heard this night, my daughter," he said to me. "But perhaps you've learned your lesson. Perhaps you'll no longer listen to conversations not intended for your ears." He walked right through the room and, without another word to anyone, let himself out through the back door.

"What is it?" my oldest sister, Fatimah, asked me urgently. "What is it? Tell us what they said. Why is my father so angry?" I didn't blame her for her surprise. Our father was often melancholy, but almost never harsh or unkind.

"My uncle thinks you're the most beautiful of the seven of us," I replied. "Aren't you pleased?"

"It's kind of him to say so," Fatimah said, preening a little. My uncle was right on that issue at least. Fatimah was certainly the handsomest. She wasn't skinny and flat, like me.

My mother agreed. "He only speaks the truth," she said. "There's no cause for anger in that."

"But he wouldn't allow his sons to marry one of us if we were the last girls on earth," I explained, keeping all emotion out of my voice. "He and his sons have no use for poor brides, even if they are cousins. The ties of blood don't mean anything to them. And to hear this my father had to humble himself."

"Did Hassan speak so," my mother asked, "even Hassan?" She hadn't been blind to our childhood friendship.

"Hassan even more than his father," I cried, dropping my pretense of control. "Don't mention Hassan to me. I don't ever want to hear his name again."

Suddenly, Fatimah began to cry. Darirah, who was much the youngest, crept close to her and put her arms about her. Sharifah and Aminah stared at her, fear in their faces. Fatimah was always cheerful, always serene. If even Fatimah was weeping, there could be no joy left anywhere in Baghdad.

"Please, Fatimah, don't cry," Sharifah begged. "Please, stop crying."

"There's no reason to cry," Zaynab added sternly. She was the second to the oldest and the one most like my mother.

But my mother knew why Fatimah was crying, even if Zaynab didn't, and my mother spoke to her in a far gentler tone than was customary with her. "Don't weep, my daughter," she said. "Allah will provide a husband for you. He provided one for me, who came from a poor family too, and he'll provide one for you. We must place our faith in Allah and not complain."

Fatimah sniffed back her tears. "I always believed that, my mother. I always believed that with my whole heart. But tonight I wonder what they'll be like, those husbands that Allah will provide for us." And I knew what she was thinking. I knew what all of my sisters

15

were thinking. They were thinking the thoughts that until this night they'd been able to push down to the bottom of their minds. Who were the husbands of girls without money? Poor farmers from the country, for whom a wife was a beast of burden, cheaper to feed than a donkey. Rich old men, who already had two or three others, and were looking now for a very young one to warm their ancient bones and to further increase the consequence of the first wife, the one who counted. Thieves and assassins who sought women with no family, or with families powerless to protect their daughters from whatever abominations their husbands chose to inflict upon them.

"Think of your father," my mother said. "Think of him. He's my husband, and he took me though I came to him with nothing. Could I have gotten a better husband if I had brought with me gifts worth a thousand dinars?"

My sisters were silent. They suspected that there was no other man in all the land between the two rivers like my father. And my mother, my mother knew it for a fact.

Long after we were all supposed to be asleep on the roof, we heard my mother and my father talking together in the courtyard below us. They kept their voices soft enough so that we couldn't catch their words, but we understood the tone. My mother was very angry; my father was very worried.

One by one, my sisters drifted off. Still I could hear my mother and my father talking, discussing, arguing, and then beginning all over again. When at last my own eyelids were so heavy with sleep that even my swirling brain couldn't keep them from closing, I could still hear, as I sank into slumber, the rise and fall of their voices.

SPRING PASSED INTO SUMMER, summer turned into autumn. Then came winter, and the rain. Every morning my uncle came to visit my father in my father's little shop. Of course, I was never there, but I knew what took place. My father told me. It was always the same.

"Good morning, O father of girls," my uncle would greet him with a sneer. "How do you feel today, Abu al-Banat?" And then he would talk about the shipment of silks and spices he had just received from Hassan, or the packet of gold Ali had dispatched through a trusted messenger. "Allah has blessed me beyond my deserving," he would always continue. "It's a wonderful thing to be the father of sons. Because of them, I prosper beyond my wildest dreams." As if it were an afterthought, he'd add, "And how are your beautiful daughters, O my brother? Have you found husbands for any of them yet?" He would laugh with a pretense of good humor. "If you don't find husbands for them soon, they'll be too old. Even the garbage collectors won't want them."

All my father ever said in reply was, "My seven daughters make my house like Paradise. Allah has blessed me too, O my brother. May he continue to shower his bounty upon you and your sons all your days."

"Oh, he will, he will," my uncle would answer complacently. "Why shouldn't he? Things will get better for you someday too. Wait and see. Wait and see."

One by one my cousins left Baghdad for other cities. After the disaster of Hassan's farewell to my father, the other boys didn't come to our house prior to their departures. They said goodbye at the shop, which suited my mother very well. There my father served them yogurt and water, but he wasn't expected to give them anything to eat. He never again mentioned the wisdom of their marrying before they left Baghdad, and they were all bachelors, as we were maids. According to my uncle, he was positively besieged by matchmakers and eager parents, offering brides for his sons. He didn't neglect to describe every one of them to my father in endless detail. "The girl is as beautiful as the sun and as rich as Croesus, but Ibrahim (or Hassan, or Ali) doesn't wish to marry until he's made all the money he can in Sidon (or Alexandria or Cyprus) and comes back to Baghdad. It wouldn't be kind to take the girl so far from her family. Besides, you know these young bucks," he'd add with a wink. "They need a chance to kick up their heels a little bit if they're to make good husbands, like you and me, when the time is right."

Once again, spring came. Once again the scent of jasmine filled our courtyard. Once again my father and I sat in the deepening dusk, playing chess.

"Check," I cried. "Check, and mate." I lifted my eyes from the board and peered at him through the dimness. "Father, what's the matter with you tonight? You haven't paid any attention to this game at all. That's why I won so easily."

"You always win," he said, only this time there wasn't a hint in his voice of the secret pride he took in my skill, only a deep melancholy. "What difference does it make if you win with difficulty or easily? And of what use are all your victories?"

I went to him, kneeling beside him and taking his hand in mine. "O my father, my beloved father, please tell me what's troubling you. Please tell me why you're so sad."

"It's nothing, my child," he replied gently. "Nothing. Your uncle came to the shop today, as he always does. He bragged about his sons and his wealth, as he always does. Nothing is any different today from any other day."

"And that's the trouble," I guessed.

"You're very wise, Buran," he said. "You should have been born a man."

"Yes," I replied, letting out a little of the bitterness that had festered inside of me for as long as I could remember. "If I were a man, I could help you. I could help my sisters. I could help myself. You know I'm as able as any man. It isn't fair. My being born a girl was a mistake."

It wouldn't have been a mistake three hundred years before, or two hundred years before, or even a hundred years before. I'd learned that from the books my father borrowed from my uncle and let me read too. Had not Shahrazad kept herself alive through a thousand and one nights by virtue of her cleverness and knowledge, to become the beloved and long-lived queen of the sultan Shahriah? Had not Buran, for whom I was named, influenced the policies of the caliph himself? Once women had been musicians, scholars, warriors, poets, and merchants. But the descendants of the caliphs who'd founded Baghdad forgot their desert heritage. Addicted to nothing but luxury, they'd permitted actual power to fall into the hands of Persian conquerors, who brought with them their own customs, including the hijab, the veil for women. It was their way of distinguishing free women from concubines. Turks had followed Persians, but the veil remained. In the end, of course, all women wore it, and none of them were free.

Perhaps my father guessed my thoughts. After all, he'd read the same books I had. He withdrew his hand from mine and patted my head. "Only the young expect life to be fair," he said. "But I love you just the way you are. I wouldn't want you to be anyone but my Buran. I'm only trying to say that if you were a man, I wouldn't have to worry about you so much. That's all."

"You don't have to worry about me now," I answered quietly. Surrounded by the darkness, so that he couldn't see my face, nor I his, I was ready to tell him about my secret dream.

But the moment passed. Abruptly he stood up. "I certainly do have to worry about you," he said, almost angrily. "I have to worry about you, and Fatimah, and Zaynab, and Khalidah, and Sharifah, and Aminah, and Darirah." Rapidly he paced from one side of the little courtyard to the other. "What's to become of you? When I die, who'll take care of you? I have nothing to leave you. I can't afford to insure you decent husbands. So far I've resisted the inevitable. I haven't let you go in marriage to men who're not good enough for you. I haven't sent you to be servants in other people's houses. But when I die, how are you going to avoid those fates?" As suddenly as he had risen, he sat down again. "O my daughter." He sighed. "Forgive me. I hadn't meant to speak to you of such things. I didn't want to spoil the even tenor of your days. I wanted you to be content and cheerful for as long as possible."

He, who knew me so well, didn't know me at all.

"O father," I murmured, "I'm not content and I'm not cheerful. You and my mother don't have to carry this burden alone. I think about my future too, and my sisters'. I think about it often. I worry about it. I know what the situation is. What made you imagine I didn't?"

"You understand too much, Buran."

"No," I cried. "No. If I didn't know the truth, what could I do to help?"

"What can you do to help anyway?" my father replied quietly. "So it would be better if you didn't know."

"Even my sisters know," I said. "Even they think about it and worry about it." It was my turn to stand up. I moved a little away from him and turned to confront him, though I couldn't see the expression on his face. "As for me," I said, "I've thought about it so much that I've even come up with a solution." Now he would listen. Now I would tell him my secret dream.

"A solution?" he said. "What kind of solution? The only solution is to beg from your uncle. I'd do it, too, no matter how much it hurt to swallow my pride, if I thought there was any hope of help from that quarter. But since there isn't, I don't need to humiliate myself."

"Calm yourself, father," I said. "I'll go in and get a lamp." I entered the house. The night was warm for so early in the season, and my sisters had gone up to the roof to catch the breeze. My mother was alone in the room. "Come out with me, my mother," I said. "I want you to hear what I'm about to say to my father."

"I haven't time for chitchat," my mother said impatiently. But I picked up the lamp from the low table on which it was set. It was the only lamp in the room. My mother had no choice but to follow me through the iwan into the courtyard. I placed the lamp on the chess table. I sat on the mat of woven date leaves between my father and my mother, my knees drawn up and my arms around them. I felt that I would have the courage to say what I was going to say if I held on to myself.

"Well," said my mother, "what's this all about? It had better be something important for you to take my lamp from me while I was sewing." But she was sewing still, having scarcely lost a stitch in the move from the house to the court.

"Buran thinks she can find wedding money for herself and her sisters," my father said drily. "I can't think how, except by selling herself. I'd kill her before I'd let her do that."

"And I'd kill myself before I'd do anything dishonorable," I assured him.

"Well, all that goes without saying," my ever-practical mother said. She had no use for dreams or philosophy. "We know, Buran, what's not to be done. Now you may tell us what *is* to be done." Her voice was hard with sarcasm. It didn't surprise her, as it had my father, that I knew of their worries. She and I talked of little else. Still, I had never said to her what I was now about to say.

"O my father, O my mother, you know that I'm as clever as my cousins."

"Far cleverer," my mother responded with a shrug. "So what good does it do you? What can you buy with clever?"

"Clever can get us what we need," I returned, careful to keep my voice and my eyes respectful. "Father, you have a little bit of money hidden away, just a small amount. You've told me that."

My father nodded. "It's for your mother. When I go, at least she'll be provided for."

"Risk it, Father, risk it," I urged. "It'll be no risk."

"In what do you want me to invest it, my child?" he asked. "I've thought of it, but I haven't discovered anything safe enough. I don't dare lose it. Your mother and I have gone to bed with an empty stomach more than one night in order to accumulate even such a tiny store."

"Invest it in me, Father," I whispered.

His eyes narrowed, his forehead creased with a frown. "Buran, what do you mean?"

Now we had come to the kernel. My hands were shaking, but I clasped them so tightly no one could see that. I made my voice strong and firm. "I want to do

24

what my cousins have done. I've always dreamed of it. I'm as smart as they are. Send me to one of the cities along the coast. With the money, I'll set up shop. Those seaports are full of sailors. They sell their goods cheap, they're so eager to get rid of them. And merchants come, on caravan, just as eager to buy. I'll send what I make to you. You'll be rich in a few months' time. My uncle will be as nothing compared to you."

At first my parents were so flabbergasted they couldn't speak. That's why I was able to say so much without being interrupted. My mother recovered her voice first. "Tomorrow I'll send for that old woman who lives in the Muqtadiyya district. She makes a secret broth from a certain herb she finds in the desert. It's said to cure madness."

"Mother, I'm not mad."

"Yes, you are." She spoke as calmly as if she were discussing the purchase of a cooking pot. "If the old woman's elixir can't cure you, your sisters and I will raise a great lamentation and rend our clothing, mourning for your lost reason."

"Mother, listen to me. I'm not mad."

She opened her mouth to speak again, but my father said sharply, "Be quiet, wife." And then he said to me, "You're not mad, Buran, but like me, you're a dreamer. You dream of things that cannot be."

My mother couldn't be silenced for long. "Women don't go into business." She uttered the words like a pronouncement.

25

"They sell vegetables in the bazaar," I pointed out. "I see them every time I go there."

"If they must. If their husbands or fathers can't support them. But they're certainly not merchants or traders, like your uncles and his sons. In the history of the world, such a thing has never happened."

"O my mother, that's not true," I protested. "Things were different once, and they don't have to be the way they are now forever."

"We don't live in some other place or some other time," she retorted. "We live here and now. Here and now, where one of his daughters in the suq would be a disgrace to your father. He can scarcely hold his head up as it is."

"It'll be a disgrace only if I fail," I said. "I will not fail."

My mother turned to my father. "You could beat her," she said. "If the old woman's elixir doesn't work, you could beat her. Beating is one of the best methods for driving out evil spirits."

I acted as if I hadn't heard her. "No one need even know," I said. "I'm thin; my breasts are small. I'll dress as a young man. I'll take a man's name. It'll be a secret between the three of us."

"And your sisters? What will we say to your sisters?" my father asked. I felt a stab of joy in my heart when I heard those words. He was talking now as if the idea was something other than a dream, as if it was a matter to be seriously considered, its virtues and flaws to be carefully weighed. His question gave it reality.

"You'll tell them I'm going to be a servant in a rich man's house. You can tell that to my uncle too, if you want."

"A disgrace, a disgrace," my mother moaned.

"Honest work isn't a disgrace," my father remonstrated.

"But she won't be doing honest work," my mother pointed out.

"What I'm really doing is just what no one will know," I said. "And it will be honest work. Just because a thing hasn't been done doesn't mean it isn't honest."

"It's out of the question," my father said. "It's totally and absolutely out of the question."

"But Father," I cried, "you can't mean that. You just said. . . ."

He shook his head. "We won't speak of it again."

"Please, Father. . . ."

He stood up. "Buran, you're pushing me too far. If you don't keep quiet, I'll do as your mother suggested. I'll beat you. Don't ever mention this matter again. I've indulged you in every wild fancy all your life. I can see how that was a mistake. From now on, you'll tend to your sewing and your baking and your weaving, like a good girl." He put his hand on my mother's shoulder. "Come, wife. It's time for us to go to bed."

She rose too. They crossed the courtyard and entered the iwan. My mother turned in the arch and said, "Bring in the lamp, Buran, and put it out." That was all. Not even, "Sleep well, my child."

The next week was the worst of my life. Nothing before or after was ever as bleak or as hopeless as that time during which my father withdrew himself from me. There was nothing in me or in my surroundings to make up for the absence of his companionship. We didn't play chess. We didn't read together the ancient tales of jinns and magic carpets in the dusty volumes he borrowed from my uncle. We didn't sit in the courtyard in the twilight talking about what had gone on that day in his shop, while he fingered his beads and I ground spices in my mother's mortar. If he had had a son, he would never have talked to me about business, or read stories to me, or taught me chess. I would never have known what I was missing. But to have my life's greatest pleasure snatched away from me, suddenly and unjustly, and with no promise of its return, was more than I could bear. I raged and I wept, but only inside of myself, where no one could see. My sisters had no idea of what I had lost. My mother had no sympathy for it. As for my father, I couldn't talk to him. He didn't reply to any words of mine. He greeted me in the morning, as he greeted all the others, and he wished me a good night, as he wished all the others. That was all.

Then something even worse happened. He became ill. A fever laid him low and for two weeks my mother, Fatimah, and Zaynab took turns nursing him. I wasn't invited to assist them, and my father didn't ask for me. They bought herbs with which to brew healing broths and potions, but when their mixtures did no good, they sent for my uncle. He paid a barber to come. Naturally, he wasn't the best barber in Baghdad. His leeches and unguents proved of no use either. My uncle suggested that we take my father to al-Maristan, the hospital, which cost nothing. My father refused to go. "If I die, let me die among those I love," he said.

The fever had simply to run its course, and the fact that it left my father no worse than pale and weak was due entirely to the care my mother, Fatimah, and Zaynab gave him. Day and night they sponged his body with cool water. They spooned hot soup down his unwilling throat. They wrapped him in piles of blankets when he shivered and unwrapped him again when he grew warm. Thus the fever did no permanent damage to his mind or to his senses. In time, his strength would return, and he would be as he had been.

But meanwhile, he sat in the courtyard in the shade from the narrow roof that extended a little bit beyond the house. He nibbled at the jellies and the boiled chicken my mother prepared to tempt his sadly diminished appetite. Every day my uncle called at our house to inquire how he did. I wished he wouldn't come. I don't know what they spoke about. I was, of course, indoors at the time, and I'd given up the habit of eavesdropping. But I did know that his visits always left my father depressed and unhappy, making his recovery slower than it had to be.

One day, after my uncle left, my mother dispatched Zaynab into the court to sit with my father, to tend to him, to fetch what he needed, and to keep him company. In another time, that would have been my task.

But Zaynab wasn't with him very long. A few minutes after she'd gone out, she came back into the house. "My father wants Buran," she said. "I don't know why." She sounded put out. She knew I was in disgrace, though she didn't know the reason, and she had enjoyed her new role as my replacement. If things kept on as they had been going just before my father fell ill, in time he might teach her to read and write, as he had taught me. If I was to return to favor, she would lose her chance. She was the only one beside me who wanted it.

But my father had asked for me, and she was forced to carry the message. I hurried out into the courtyard as soon as she had spoken.

A few cushions had been arranged against the wall of the house. His head rested against them, and his eyes, deep in gray sockets, were shut. If he was actually sleeping, I didn't want to disturb him. He needed rest. When I stood next to him, I whispered softly, "O my father."

He wasn't asleep. His eyelids flew open. "Buran," he said quietly. His hand reached for mine. "Sit down beside me." He spoke as if there had never been any difficulty between us.

At first, after I had seated myself next to him, he didn't say anything. His eyes just examined my face for a long time. It was as if by looking at me he thought he could ferret out the truth of my soul. Perhaps he could. At last he spoke. "Buran, I have made up my mind. I have no choice but to follow your suggestion."

"O my father!" I exclaimed. But he held up his hand, bidding me be silent.

"Your mother remains very much against the whole idea," he said. "But that's neither here nor there. She can't prevent your going. Only I can do that, and I'll no longer stand in your way." He shook his head slowly. "Not that I want you to go. I think it's the scheme of a madwoman. I think I'll never see you again. But what else am I to do? It's our only chance. We have nothing to lose—except you."

"No, Father, I'll come back to you dressed in silks and jewels. Wait and see." I was exultant. I was sure. I knew that Allah was with me.

"No one knows his kismet, Buran," he warned. "No one knows his fate. Do you see how I was struck down when I least expected it—I, who never before had suffered from so much as a headache? The next time, perhaps, I won't recover. . . ."

"Father," I begged, "don't speak of such things."

"Why not, Buran?" he asked. "You're the one who's so keen to face the truth. Which one of us can foresee the future? I thought I had time, but maybe I don't." His voice was low and intense. "Perhaps Allah inflicted this illness upon me. Perhaps he wants me to understand the fragility of any man's hold on life. I can't even count on myself to provide for you while I'm still alive. The shop's been closed for three weeks. For three weeks I haven't brought a single durham into this house. Suppose I was permanently disabled in some way? That would be worse than my dying. You would have the added burden of taking care of me."

I didn't contradict what he was saying. It was true, and his realization of it was what had persuaded him to give me my chance.

He lifted his hand and pointed to the corner where the house met the wall. "If you kneel there," he said, "and feel about with your hands, you'll discover a loose brick. Lift up the brick and bring me what you find."

I did as he instructed. Beneath the brick I discovered a little pouch of worn dark leather. I carried it to him and put it in his hand. He pulled on the drawstrings to open it. "Hold out your palms," he said. I made a cup of them, and he poured out the contents of the little bag. "Count them," he instructed.

I counted them.

"How much is there?" he asked.

"Fifteen dinars and seven durhams," I replied.

He nodded. "We had sixteen dinars before I got sick. Your mother broke one to buy the expensive tidbits she thinks I need. What's left of it will last awhile yet, until I'm back at the shop. You'll take what's here with you." He ran his fingers through the little pile on my lap. "So few." He sighed. "So few for a lifetime's labor. Not enough to do any of us any good. From such a scrawny pile I couldn't even make decent weddings for the lot of you, let alone give you marriage gifts sufficient for a respectable match."

"It's enough, Father," I said. "It's enough. It will come back to you a thousand times." Carefully I slipped each coin back into the bag. I pulled the drawstrings tight, and then I dropped the bag into the pocket of my sarwal, my trousers.

Later, after my sisters had gone to bed and my father had fallen into the light, easy sleep of convalescence, my mother and I talked. "I don't want you to go," she said. "It's wrong to fly in the face of custom. Each of us has a place, and if we fall out of it, the world will turn upside down. But your father's set on your going now, and you're set on it too. I don't think I'll ever see you again, but I won't withhold my blessing from you."

33

"Thank you, my mother," I said. "I couldn't go without it. But you'll see me again. Don't worry." I told her a story. My mother loved stories. "The summer sun will turn the garden into dust," I said. "Fall will come, and with it the cool winds from the west. Winter rains will fall on the city and fill the canals to the brim. Then spring will be here once more, with the scent of jasmine, and then the dry, dusty summer, and then the cool winds of fall. When the autumn winds blow yet a third time, then I too will come again."

My mother shook her head. She didn't believe me. But she accepted my going. She believed in kismet, in fate. What was going to happen would happen. There was nothing anyone could do about it. As for me, I know you can't avoid your kismet. But I also know you can help it along a little.

The next day I covered my face with my hijab, as does any modest woman when she leaves the house. I was being perfectly attentive to custom at the very moment that I was hatching plans to flout it completely. But I didn't think about that irony then. I was too busy to think. I had time only to act.

I went to the suq nearest our house, a poor bazaar befitting a poor neighborhood. The narrow, unpaved street was lined on both sides with tiny shops connected to each other beneath a long arcade. It was late, the sun was close to setting, and the tradesmen were beginning to think about home and supper. It was the hour at which to buy goods cheap.

The shop of Abu Ishaq sold second-hand clothing. It would be cheaper to make what I needed, but I didn't have the time. I selected wide pantaloons, a vest, a loose-fitting shirt, stockings, pointed shoes, a fez, a white linen money belt, and a handsome striped cotton jubba to cover all, and to cover me too. I told the shopkeeper they were for my brother. "He's about my height," I said. "I think these things will fit him, don't you?"

"Certainly, daughter," the stall keeper responded with a little bow. "You have a most educated eye, daughter. You've selected the very finest items I have for sale. They belonged to a rich man's son. He wears a garment once and then he discards it for a new one. You couldn't have made a better choice."

The man was lying. Except for the jubba, all the items I'd picked out had places on them where the material was worn thin with age. But that didn't matter. The jubba, which was in excellent condition, would hide everything else most of the time.

"You see, uncle," I pointed out, "you see where the material is worn thin here? The rich man's son must have let his servants wear the clothes before he had them sent over to you."

"Impossible," the shopkeeper insisted. "That's just the way the material is woven. You won't find a better piece of goods in Baghdad." But his heart wasn't in the bargaining. It was late, and he wanted to get home. I sobbed a little when I told him how poor we were, and how we never thought to see our dear brother again, for our poverty had forced us to put him into service with a distant cousin in Damascus.

"Then he leaves with the caravan tomorrow?" the stall keeper asked.

Tomorrow? Tomorrow? Tuesday? I was glad to discover that a caravan was scheduled to depart the very next day. As my father always said, whatever you wanted to know, you had only to go to the bazaar to find out. "Yes," I said, "the one that leaves tomorrow from the khan by al-Maristan."

"No, no, not from the khan by al-Maristan, child," the stall keeper said patronizingly. "It leaves from the khan at the end of Suq al-Thalatha, promptly at first light. It's led by Gindar the African, and he's very strict with all who travel in his company."

"Yes, yes, of course," I agreed. "Gindar the African. We had to give him two dinars to take my brother."

"Two dinars?" the stall keeper cried. "Two dinars? I'm through bargaining with you. You're better at it than I am. If your father could persuade Gindar the Strict to take your brother for only two dinars, I won't get anywhere with you. Take everything, take it all. Take it for eleven durhams."

"Three durhams."

"Nine durhams."

"Five durhams."

"Seven durhams."

"Done."

"And done."

I bundled the clothes together quickly and left before he could change his mind. I was satisfied. I had acquired a man's entire wardrobe and all the information I needed for only seven durhams. I thought my success was a good omen for the future.

The next morning I arose long before daybreak. My sisters were still asleep. I hadn't said goodbye to them the night before. They weren't to know what I was really doing. My mother would tell them later that I'd gone to be a servant in a rich man's house and that I was so miserable over my fate that I hadn't been able to bring myself to make them a proper farewell.

So I said goodbye to each one of them as they lay sleeping. I said goodbye in my heart. "Goodbye, Fatimah," I thought. "I'll see to it that you find a husband worthy of your loveliness. Goodbye, Zaynab. Be a good friend to my father while I'm gone. Goodbye, Khalidah. Don't gossip about me when you go to the well, because you won't be telling the truth. Goodbye, Sharifah. Tell my mother to give you the comb and the mirror I left behind. I won't be needing them where I'm going. Goodbye, Aminah. Take good care of little Darirah, because she's soft-hearted and will cry the most for me when I'm gone." But to Darirah I couldn't say goodbye, not even silently, because I knew that if I did, I'd run over to her and take her in my arms and cover her sweet, tiny face with kisses. She would wake, and the others would wake, and I'd surely miss Gindar the Strict and his caravan.

My mother and father were waiting for me in the other room. My mother kissed me. "May Allah watch over you, my child," she said. Into my hand she pressed a goatskin flask and a packet of flat loaves of bread. She must have stayed up most of the night baking them. There were enough to keep me almost all the way to the coast. That would save me a lot of money. Food was expensive on caravan.

My father had something for me too. It was the carved white ivory queen from his precious chess set. "The king is lost if the queen is taken," he said. "I won't play chess until you come home again."

I put the piece in my money belt. "It's my talisman," I said, "my treasure. As long as I have it, I know I'll be safe."

My father kissed me, too, on each cheek. "May Allah protect you," he said. "May he protect you and shower his blessings upon you."

"And upon you, O my father," I whispered. I kissed them both once again, my mother and my father, and then I left the house as quickly as I could. If I had stayed any longer, my nerve might have deserted me. I hadn't known in advance how hard it was going to be to say goodbye. My dream was coming true, and already I knew that wasn't an unmixed blessing.

Though my parents realized I intended to disguise myself as a boy, actually seeing me in men's clothing would have been more of a shock than they could have borne, so I hadn't put on the garments I'd purchased before I'd said goodbye to them. It was time to put them on now. And since it isn't manly to cry, I forced my tears back of my eyes and wiped from my cheeks the ones that had already fallen. In the courtyard, I hacked off my hair with a scissors. I didn't have to do a perfect job. My felt hat would cover my head completely anyway.

Swiftly I pulled on my new clothes. I left the old ones in a little pile beneath the blooming jasmine. I would have no use for them on my travels, or after I came again, rich and dressed in silk. I left my mother's scissors there, too.

Beneath my shirt and vest, I bound my money belt tightly around my waist. A thief would have to murder me to get it, and I wasn't dressed richly enough to be worth murdering. Besides, traveling with Gindar the African was supposed to be safe. Traveling with him would also sadly reduce my store of money, but there wasn't anything I could do about that.

I slipped out of the gate, hoping I had at least an hour until first light. I strode swiftly through the narrow, winding streets. Occasionally, a dog barked at me. I passed a woodcutter carrying a load of sticks on his back and a farmer leading a donkey loaded with palm rib boxes full of chickens. A dairyman with two pails yoked over his shoulders jostled me as I went by.

It was still dark, but already buyers and sellers from outlying villages had begun to trade. No one gave me a second glance. My disguise was working. I was just a boy and, like everyone else, merely on my way through the dusty, crooked streets of the Suq al-Thalatha, the Tuesday market, the oldest and longest bazaar on the Rasafa, the eastern side of the Tigris River.

A bend in the suq brought me to the handsome buildings of Nizamiyya College, newly built by our Turkish masters for the study of theology. The golden age was past; there were no women students at the Nizamiyya College. I stood at the curb, facing the wide, well-tended Great Road, which ran along the bank of the river to one of the nine gates in the wall that surrounded the Dar al-Khalifa, the caliphs' palaces. Behind those walls, the caliphs built magnificent dwellings, tended luxurious gardens full of exotic imported plants, played polo, hunted lions and cheetahs, raised horses, and indulged themselves in who knows what unimaginable abominations. They had wandered far from the path proscribed by the prophet Mohammed in the holy Koran, and now it was not they, but the Turkish Suljuq sultans, who truly ruled the land between two rivers.

The sun rose. The walls, the gate, the palm trees glowed rose and gold. The voices of the muezzins on the minarets within and without the wall called believers everywhere to prayer.

Allahu akbar. Allahu akbar,
La ilaha illa Allah.

God is great, God is great,
There is no god but God.

When would I see my beautiful city again? When would I again walk the streets of home? I had promised my mother that I would return after three summers had come and gone. But even as I'd spoken, I'd known I was making a promise that was perhaps beyond my power to keep.

I hurried on. Around the last bend of the suq, I came to the khan—the inn, the caravansary, where caravans gathered, where they rested on their way, and where most of the wholesale business of cities was conducted.

The wide gate stood open. I peeked inside. The courtyard was jammed with men—white men, yellow men, black men, tan men. Some were dressed like the men I knew, like me myself. Others wore outlandish costumes in colors of which I'd only dreamed. Still others covered their bodies with almost nothing at all. The din of their voices filled my ears, but I couldn't understand anything I heard. Their languages were as varied as their dress and their skin.

I drew back outside the gate. Where was I to go? To whom was I to speak? I felt as lost as a fledgling that's fallen from the nest. The smart thing to do, I

PART ONE

thought, was simply to turn around and go home. This
was no place for Buran, sheltered and protected daughter of that Malik who was known throughout Baghdad
as Abu al-Banat.

Next to the gate, built into the wall, was a great
tank hewn out of stone and kept full of water for the
benefit of all who passed, thanks to an endowment
left by a wealthy citizen insuring through blessed
charity his place in Paradise. I pushed aside the marble
lid, filled the copper ladle fastened firmly to the lid
with a chain, and drank the cold water until I was
satisfied. It seemed to fill me with courage as it
quenched my thirst.

This was no place for Buran, but it was the right
place, the only place, for Nasir, self-created that very
morning and out to make his own way in the world.
I threw back my shoulders, thrust out my chin, and
stepped forward through the gate with just a touch of
a swagger, much like the one I had seen in the walk
of Hassan as I'd peered at him through curtains and
arches half a hundred times.

A few men were squatting on benches of baked
bricks on both sides of the gate. I picked out the one
with the kindest-looking face and approached him.
"Alsalamu alaykum. Peace be with you," I greeted
him.

"And to you, son," he answered.

"I seek a place in the caravan," I said, dispensing
with any further formalities.

"Then go find Gindar the Rayyis, the chief, or you won't make the journey," the man warned me. "You can't miss him," he added with a laugh. Then he turned away to talk to his neighbor.

I stepped down into the huge open courtyard. I was swallowed up in the melee. Horses, donkeys, camels, and shepherd dogs neighed and hee-hawed and barked. The beaten dirt of the ground was covered with bales of merchandise, stuffed saddle bags, packages wrapped in leather, and countless other bundles in the process of being loaded on the backs of animals. I had come just in time. In another half an hour, the caravan would have departed, leaving nothing in the courtyard but piles of dung for the porters to clean away before the arrival of the next caravan, the next crowd of merchants and traders.

I stepped through a door into the vast inner, roofed courtyard. It was just as crowded with human beings as the outer area, but it was at least free of animals. All around, above and below, doors opened into it from the countless rooms where the travelers lodged. I went from one chattering group of men to another, but not one man I saw looked to me like the rayyis. In my mind I carried a picture of Gindar the Chief, and though the realities I had so far encountered were like nothing I'd imagined, I was still wedded to the images inside of my own head.

Once again in the outer courtyard, I approached a camel driver singing softly to himself as he slung a

houdaj over a kneeling animal. His white teeth sparkled in his dark, shining face, and he had a cheerful
gleam in his bright black eyes. I mustered up the courage I needed to speak to him. Since the day I had
become a woman, he and the man sitting at the gate
were the first men other than my father to whom I'd
spoken without wearing a hijab that covered my face.
But, I reminded myself, now I was not a woman. I was
Nasir.

"Pardon me, Uncle," I called out in a tone that I
hoped was both good-natured and slightly condescending. He was only a camel driver, after all, and I was
supposed to be a traveling merchant. "Can you assist
me with some directions?"

"Certainly, my son," the driver responded.
"What do you want to know?"

"Where can I find the leader of this caravan?" I
asked. "Where can I find that fearful horseman,
Gindar the Chief?"

With a light touch on the camel's knees, the
driver persuaded the animal to rise. Then he turned
his full attention to me. "What do you want him for,
my son?" he asked.

I drew myself up to my full height. "What business is that of yours, camel-driver?" I asked haughtily.

He smiled. "Now, now, don't get uppity, my son.
It certainly is my business, for I'm that fearful horseman, Gindar the Chief." His eyes shone with laughter.

"I'm also a fearful camel driver, a fearful marksman, and even a fearful camp cook, if the need arises."

"Pardon me, honored chief," I murmured, ducking my head with sudden politeness. But I wasn't afraid. It was impossible to be afraid of such a cheerful man, even though his broad shoulders and six feet or more of height suggested that he wasn't the sort of person one would care to have for an enemy. "My mistake was perhaps understandable."

Gindar stood very close to me, his imposing figure making me feel positively scrawny. "Do you wish to join my caravan?" he asked.

I nodded mutely.

"You've never traveled caravan before," he said. It was a statement, not a question.

"That's true," I admitted.

"Then you must understand," he continued, "that on my caravan the ranks and classes that are so important in cities count for nothing. We're all equal, because the safety of all depends on the cooperation of all. If you travel with me, you treat everyone else in the group as if he were the sultan in disguise—as indeed he might be." His eyes narrowed as he looked me up and down. "A man on my caravan will tell you as much about himself as he wants you to know. Don't ask him any questions, and he won't ask you any."

I nodded. That suited me just fine. "What's the fee?" I asked.

"You come too late," he replied briskly. He saw the shocked look on my face and smiled a little, as if he'd planned the whole exchange to achieve just that effect. "I'm all filled up. Yusuf ibn-Beker leads another caravan to the coast in a couple of days. Wait for him."

"What do you mean, you're all filled up?" I cried. "How can that be? What difference does it make if another person comes along?"

"Don't speak foolishly, my son," he said, the patronizing manner all on his side now. "I can carry only so much food; and besides if there are too many people, someone always manages to get lost."

"I'm only one. . . ." I begged. I couldn't wait. I couldn't go back home with my hair cut short and my women's clothes abandoned and my sisters believing a fib about my having gone to be a servant. I couldn't hang around Baghdad all by myself either. I'd use up too much money and run the risk of being recognized. The enormous sense of self-congratulation that had possessed me the day before as I'd come home from shopping in the suq was all gone now.

Still, there was nothing for it but to go forward. I fell to my knees. "Please, please, honored chief, take me with you. It's essential that I leave Baghdad today. I have some food of my own. Your cook and your baker won't have to prepare anything for me. I'm such a small, unimportant person, I'll take up no significant space. I'll sleep in the open; I'll travel the whole distance on foot; I'll be very good about keeping up. I beg you, honored chief, take me with you."

"Get up, silly boy," he said, putting his hand on my upper arm and lifting me, willy-nilly, to my feet. "I told you, we're all equal here. No one has to grovel before Gindar the African. No one ever accused me of having a hard heart, either. If it's so important to you, then you may come. It'll cost you five dinars."

"Five dinars!" I was flabbergasted. If I gave Gindar five dinars, I would be left with only nine. I couldn't even live in a town for more than a few months, let alone set up shop, with just nine dinars in my pouch. It was impossible. Why hadn't I asked my father to investigate these details more thoroughly? Why had I imagined that a caravan journey all the way to the sea would cost me only two dinars? Why had I supposed that what I imagined was what was true? I was faint with the sudden realization of my own ignorance, my own naivete.

Without a word, I turned away from Gindar and began to pick my way among the noisy, milling crowd, back to the gate. I would go home. I would go home not two hours after I'd left, confess my failure, take off my jubba, put on my hijab, wait for my hair to grow back, and then, in penance, truly go for a servant in a rich man's house, where my maidenhood would be lost in a month's time, considered by my employer justified compensation for my lack of skill at housewifely tasks.

So bleak was that prospect that another thought occurred to me. It would be better to attempt to cross the desert by myself and die on the journey, my bones picked clean by vultures and left to bleach in the sun, then go back home. Anything, anything would be better than the cowardice that a return to my father's house would represent.

So I hadn't even reached the Thalatha Bridge when I turned back again. I would try Gindar the African once more before I set out on my own. Inside the caravansary, a fat merchant was mounting the camel Gindar had saddled, assisted by a ragged boy. Gindar had disappeared. But he couldn't have gone far. "Please, gracious lad," I called, remembering Gindar's stricture about the sultan in disguise, "could you tell me where Gindar the Chief has gone? It's urgent that I see him."

The boy lifted his hand to point toward the doorway leading inside, but before he could say anything, the fat man on the camel spoke. "Tend to your business, boy," he ordered sharply. "You haven't any time for gossip." Apparently the merchant had never heard Gindar's speech about the democracy of the caravan.

But I had already glimpsed Gindar in the group to which the boy had pointed. It would be impossible to miss him, his tall, dark form towered so far above the others. I hurried toward him as quickly as I could in that milling throng. I didn't want to lose sight of him again.

His back was to me when I reached him. "Honored rayyis," I said quite loudly when I was almost on top of him. It was difficult for me to speak up, but I had to in order to be heard above the din.

He turned. "You again?" he asked with a little laugh when he saw me. "Did you come back to bargain with me? I'm not a bazaar merchant. My price is my price."

"I wouldn't doubt that for a moment," I hastened to assure him. "But I must leave Baghdad. It's essential. I don't have five dinars to give you." I kept my tone and my carriage carefully polite, but proud and free. I wouldn't grovel. That wasn't a tactic to please a man like Gindar anyway. "Couldn't I travel as a servant? If not as yours, then for one of the merchants? I would do anything, anything at all, and I wouldn't ask for any pay other than my passage."

"What other pay could you expect?" Gindar asked. "What are you able to do?"

Not much that needed to be done on caravan, but I trusted the quickness of my mind to teach me. I'd already learned a lot in a very short time. "Anything," I replied firmly. "Anything at all."

A thin, long-legged, sun-browned man standing next to Gindar spoke up. "Brother," he said, "Jihha isn't satisfied with his boy, who cries day and night for his mother and his village. Jihha would be very, very happy to send the boy home and be rid of him if he had someone else to serve him."

"Me!" I cried. "Let it be me. You'll never regret it, kind sir, nor you, Chief Gindar, nor will Jihha, whoever he is."

Gindar laughed. "I see now that I can't escape. Allah has decreed that for good or ill you're meant to make this journey with us." He put his hand on the other man's shoulder. "Abu Sinan, take this lad to Jihha, and good luck to him." If I'd been listening as closely as I should have been, I would have been worried at the ironic tone in which Gindar spoke that final phrase, but I was so overjoyed at the success of my ploy that I had no room for anything in my mind but satisfaction.

"Come, lad," Abu Sinan said, "follow me."

I smiled. "Thank you, thank you, Chief Gindar." Abu Sinan was already on his way, and I hurried after him.

"Wait," Gindar called. "Wait."

I stopped. So did Abu Sinan. "You know my name," Gindar said. "What's yours?"

My mouth opened. My tongue moved to my lips. But, praise Allah, before I could form the word "Buran," my mouth snapped shut again. When I reopened it, I was able to utter smoothly, "Nasir, Chief. Nasir ibn-Malik." My father's name was so common I thought it did no harm not to lie about that at least.

"Well, child of Malik," Gindar said, "make sure

you serve Jihha well. I'm jeopardizing my reputation as a truth-speaker for your sake."

"Don't worry, honored Chief, I'll not fail you," I assured him. "I'm eternally grateful to you for your help. Allah will reward you, even if I can't."

Gindar laughed again. "We'll see if your eternal gratitude lasts as long as it takes us to get to the coast." He turned away then to tend to the loading of a donkey, appearing to forget I'd ever existed.

"Come along, lad," Abu Sinan ordered. I followed him almost at a trot in an effort to keep up with his long strides as he crossed rapidly through the camp. In a moment we were in the presence of Jihha.

I had seen Jihha before. What had happened to my luck this morning? Jihha was the very same absurdly fat man whose unfortunate servant I had spoken to a little while earlier. He still sat astride his camel. Once he'd managed to settle his enormous bulk atop the poor creature, he was forced to remain there until he dismounted for the night. For him, getting on and off a camel was not an enterprise casually undertaken.

His boy was holding the camel's reins. Jihha was screaming at the boy like a wild baboon, his face flushed red as blood, his waving arm cutting the air like a sword. "You fool, why did you force me on top of this creature, when it's obvious that this caravan won't move for another half-hour? It's lucky for you that you're down there and I'm up here, or I'd beat you within an inch of your life."

The boy turned up his tear-streaked, dirty face. "But rayyis," he moaned, "you told me to help you mount. I dared not disobey you."

The explanation didn't improve Jihha's temper. "Whatever have I done to Allah," he shouted, "that I should be cursed with such a stupid servant?"

"Jihha," Abu Sinan called, "the curse is lifted. I've brought you a new servant."

At this I bowed low. "Peace be with you, honored chief," I said.

"Straighten up, boy, so I can get a good look at you." I obeyed. The dirty-faced lad had stopped crying. He gazed at me with eyes full of such hope that he seemed to believe I was the Prophet himself, come to redeem the entire human race. "You're awfully small," said Jihha.

"But very strong, honored chief," I assured him.

"I can't afford to pay you anything while we're on caravan," he added. That was obviously a lie. He was garbed completely in silk; even his traveling vest and jacket were of silk. "Once I've traded my goods in the cities along the coast, I'll make it up to you."

He was lying again. Neither along the coast nor anywhere else would I or any other servant of his ever see so much as a durham in cash. It didn't matter. If one poor boy ran off, he could always find another to sign on in expectation of the crumbs from his table and the chance to steal something. I knew his type; my uncle was cut from the same cloth. But it didn't matter to me. I had no intention of remaining with him once I reached the coast.

Perhaps it should have mattered. Perhaps I should have given some thought in advance to what it would be like to spend six weeks or more as the servant of such a man. Perhaps I should not have once again acted so hastily. But when there isn't any choice, one must act. I now knew that I knew nothing about the world, but if I had let that stop me, I would have gone home again and nothing would ever have happened to me, at least not anything I wanted to have happen. And if I suffered too—well, when my mother said, as she did at least once a day, that nothing in life is without its price, she spoke no less than the truth.

Jihha would have let the dirty-faced boy go without any means of returning to his village, but Abu Sinan shamed him into tossing the lad a durham or two. He scrabbled for them in the dust. I was tempted to give him one of my own. However, I didn't want anyone to see that I had any money at all, not Jihha, not Abu Sinan, not anyone. But I undid my mother's packet and handed him two loaves of flat bread for his journey home. I thought I could afford to be generous. In my usual fashion, I made an assumption. I supposed that Jihha was obliged at least to feed me.

A shout resounded suddenly throughout the courtyard. The voice was so loud that it could be heard above the clangor and the din of men and animals. The surprising shriek sent a shiver down my back, but

53

then I realized it was only the public crier. "O noble travelers!" he called. "O noble travelers! With the help of Allah, we are ready to proceed."

Slowly the caravan wound out of the khan's wide gate, down the street of the suq, and across the Thalatha Bridge. We traversed the area where three hundred years before the Abbasi Caliph, Abu Ja'far al-Mansur, had built the first Baghdad, the round city known as Dar al-Salam, the city of peace. Its three walls, its great mosque, its golden palace at the heart of the circle, were gone now, destroyed by floods and storms, lightning and thunderbolts. Only the minaret and part of the gate still stood, faded but still glorious mementos of a marvelous age.

We passed al-Maristan, the hospital where my uncle had wanted my father to go when he was ill. I had never seen it before. By itself it was a whole city, rising on the ruins of the very palace where Queen Shahrazad had told her wonderful tales.

The road curved to the northwest. The caravan halted beside the great canal that flows from the Euphrates River. Abu Sinan, bringing up the rear of the caravan, pulled the rein of his camel. Gindar, on the back of the tallest camel I'd ever seen, turned toward him. The chief and his assistant galloped toward each other, conferred briefly without dismounting, and returned to their places. We moved on, crossed the bridge over the canal, and found ourselves on the green, watered plain that edges the desert.

The caravan picked up speed. All morning I walked beside Jihha's camel, my hand gripping the rope binding together the string of donkeys carrying his goods. Mile after mile we traveled beneath the blazing sun. My feet stumbled on rocks that lay across the track. Each time that happened, Jihha flicked his whip in my direction. "You clumsy fool," he shouted. "I'll lose my whole train if you aren't more careful. How stupid of me to listen to Abu Sinan and take on a fool like you." By noon, my feet were covered with blisters. My hand was sore from the pressure of the rope. I could scarcely breathe through the dust in my nostrils. My eyes were blinded from the sun's glare.

We paused for midday prayers. Abu Sinan became the muezzin, calling out, "Allahu akbar, Allahu akbar." Most of the travelers dismounted, spread small rugs on the ground, turned their faces southeast toward Mecca, and knelt to murmur seven times holy verses from the Koran. The Christian, Jewish, and Hindu merchants among us, of course, did not join the prayers. They prayed in their own way at their own times. I worshipped as the devout Moslem I never ceased to be. No matter what costume I wore, it was my duty to pray five times a day.

But Jihha didn't dismount. He was too large, and the job of getting him back on his camel would have taken too much precious time. He drank water from his goatskin flask; I drank from mine. "The third donkey carries the food," he shouted. "Bring me two

55

loaves of bread, some dates and raisins and a green onion."

I found the food, brought it back and handed it to him. I stood silently at his camel's side, staring up at him as he tore at the bread with eager fingers and stuffed half a loaf into his mouth at once. He seemed to swallow it without chewing. Only after he'd gulped down the other half did he pause long enough to look down and realize that I was still standing beneath him.

"Well, boy," he snapped, "what're you staring at? Go away."

I bowed. "Honored chief," I asked, "what food is provided for your devoted servant?" I was very hungry. I knew I couldn't expect dates or an onion. A loaf of bread would have to satisfy me. Even for half a loaf I would thank him humbly.

"Food?" Jihha cried, his face turning red with fury. "You expect me to feed you? Who are you that I should feed you? I paid Gindar for your place in this caravan. How dare you expect anything more?" If his hands hadn't been full of bread and onion, I think I would have felt the crack of his whip on my shoulders.

I turned away and went back to the donkey that was carrying my small store. I felt in the pack for my mother's loaves, but then I withdrew my hand. If I didn't want to waste a good part of my tiny fortune on food, I'd better make what I had go as far as I could. I would wait until night to eat. Bitterly, bitterly did I regret the two loaves I'd given so freely to the dirty-faced boy. I reached up and rubbed my cheek with my finger. Then I stared at the black grit that had come off on my hand. Now I too was a dirty-faced boy.

Soon the caravan started moving again. After an hour or two, I stopped feeling hot, I stopped feeling tired, I stopped feeling sore, I stopped feeling hungry. I was simply numb. The rope remained clutched in my hand because my fingers were paralyzed shut. My feet moved one in front of the other because my mind was too weary to tell them not to. When the sun glowed red on the western horizon, the caravan halted. We recited our evening prayers and then moved on again. It was not until after midnight that we came to al-Anbar, where the great canal meets the Euphrates River. We halted at last in the courtyard of the largest caravansary in the whole busy little town, swarming, like all the others, with traders and merchants from all over the world.

I was so exhausted that as soon as I stopped putting one foot in front of the other, I fell to the ground.

"Boy!" Jihha screamed. "What's the matter with you? Get me off this beast this minute or your own mother won't recognize your face if she ever sees it again."

I hoisted my aching body out of the dirt and walked over to Jihha's camel as quickly as my blistered feet would carry me. I struck the animal on the legs to make him kneel, as I had seen Gindar do that very morning. To my infinite surprise, the creature obeyed

57

me. I think I smiled then. But I really didn't know what to do next. Fortunately, there were camels kneeling all around me. I watched their drivers undo the houdajs, and then I started to imitate their movements with slow, clumsy gestures of my own.

"Now what?" Jihha complained. "Why're you looking here, looking there, like a moon calf? Tend to your business, boy. I'll teach you to take advantage of my good nature." And he cursed me with a string of curses such as I'd never dreamed our blessed language possessed. It was the first time in my life I had heard such words.

But not the last. He cursed me again when I returned from the cook's fire, carrying his supper, because he said it had taken me so long I must have dawdled on the way. And he cursed me yet again while he was eating because the food was not as hot as he thought it ought to be. Serving a meal was the one task required of me that I already knew how to do, but even so I couldn't please him.

While he ate, I unloaded all the pack animals laden with Jihha's extensive stock of wares. Again, I learned what to do by observing others. Again, it took me a very long time. When I started to work on the third donkey, the one that carried personal stores, I couldn't resist temptation. Besides, I thought that to steal food from Jihha was to take only what was my due. If I nabbed a bit to eat from him, my own supply would last one day longer. He expected it. All servants stole.

Quickly I extracted a loaf from a pack. I tore a piece from the loaf and shoved it in my mouth. At that instant I felt a huge hand grab my shoulder. Who would have thought such a mountain of a man could move as lightly and silently as a gazelle? "I caught you, thief," he shouted. "Do you think I wasn't watching you?" He shook me so hard I thought my brains would fall out through my nose.

The bread dropped out of my hands. I ran away from Jihha as fast as my sore feet would carry me, tears streaming down my cheeks, and my heart filled with envy for the dirty-faced boy who was on his way home to his village and his mother.

In the khan there was no place to hide. I darted between clumps of camels, donkeys, and men jamming the court. I ran through the gate and down the dusty, narrow road. Beyond the village, there was nothing, nothing but miles of empty wilderness. Though we were only one day out of Baghdad, to venture back myself would probably have meant death. The desert is bitter cold at night, and in the dark I'd never be able to find my way. Gindar could ask and get five dinars from those who wished to join his caravan for the simple reason that he knew the way. Alone in the desert one died surely, from the cold, or the heat, or thirst, or starvation, or the attack of wild beasts, or occasionally, in spite of the strict laws enforced by caliph and sultan, the attack of wild men.

I was out of breath. I sat down on a large boulder humping up out of the rocky soil, put my head in my hands, and wept. I think if nothing had interrupted me I might have cried until my tears washed me away, and in the morning, when the caravan moved out, someone might have noticed a little mud puddle beside the boulder, all that was left of me.

Instead, I felt something cool and soft nuzzle my lap, and when I pulled my hands away from my eyes, I saw a baby camel, his nose searching the folds of my jubba for something to eat. When he found nothing, he turned his liquid eyes up to mine, and it seemed to me that he sighed.

I actually smiled. "Ah, little one," I told him, "you and I are in the same predicament. We're both hungry. But your mother wants to feed you as much as you want to eat. Why did you wander away from her?" I stroked his rough, furry face. "Were you longing for a bit of adventure? Let me tell you something, foolish little camel. Adventure in real life is nothing like adventure in the stories Shahrazad told!"

I stood up and untied the waist cord that held my jubba closed. The camel stood still and unresisting as I fastened it about his neck. With my sleeve, I wiped my cheeks and my nose and trusted the blackness of night to hide the redness of my eyes.

I led the camel back to the khan. He probably

belonged to Gindar. Most of the animals on a caravan were supplied by the chief. I searched the groups gathered in the courtyard, hoping to recognize the form of Gindar or his vizier, Abu Sinan.

I found them together, seated with three or four merchants in the remotest corner of the inner roofed court. Servants were clearing away an elaborate meal, such as might have graced my uncle's table. Kings of the desert, like Gindar, lived well.

I approached the group slowly, still leading the litte camel. I bowed. "Pardon the interruption, Chief," I murmured, "but I found this baby wandering alone outside the town and I don't know to whom he belongs."

Gindar glanced up at me from the plate before him, laden with sweet meats. "He's not ours. A man who tethers his animals improperly deserves to lose them," he said. "But leave him here. Whoever owns him will come crying to me as soon as he notices the creature's missing." Of course that was the case. Camels were expensive. The loss of one wouldn't be taken lightly.

Gindar gestured toward Abu Sinan, as if instructing him to show me where to tie the little camel. But then, suddenly, he changed his mind and leaped to his feet himself. "Follow me," he said. "Bring the baby."

I walked behind him. We moved through the great room and out into the open court, where rows of stakes had been driven into the ground. Camels, don-

61

keys, and a couple of horses were tethered to the stakes. Other camels stood about, one of their front legs hobbled so they couldn't move far.

Gindar took the rope from my hand. As he did so, he leaned his face close to mine. "Well, Nasir, you don't look very cheerful," he said. "Jihha isn't such a pleasant employer, is he?"

"No," I agreed, "he's not."

"But it's lucky for the camel you ran outside the camp to weep for a while. If you hadn't, he'd have been lost in the desert, a jackal or a vulture's dinner."

I flushed with embarrassment. What kind of boy would Gindar imagine me to be, knowing now that I wept like a girl?

Gindar guessed my thoughts. "Don't blush, Nasir," he said quietly. "It's no disgrace for a servant of Jihha's to weep. I've never known one who didn't."

His words emboldened me. "I can't stay with him. Even if I die in the desert, I can't stay with him."

"Oh, you'll stay with him," Gindar replied, his voice cool. "You'll stay with him until we get to the coast. By then the flab on your arms will have turned to muscle. The weight on your hips will have disappeared. Your skin will have turned brown in the sun. And your head will be full of wisdom. No one will get the best of you after you've crossed the desert in the company of Jihha. Don't forget that, Nasir." Then he walked away from me, leading the camel to one of the nearby stakes. The poor creature was bleating pitifully, so hungry was he now for his mother's milk. I hoped he wouldn't have to wait long until his owner came in search of him.

I returned to Jihha and more curses. But this time I didn't cry. Words couldn't hurt me. They couldn't even insult my spirit if I didn't let them.

And the next morning, when I woke up, I found a loaf of flat bread and some dates next to my bed roll. Who could have left it there? Not Jihha, for sure. But it could have been Abu Sinan under Gindar's instructions, or Gindar himself, or one of my generous-spirited fellow travelers."

Two hours past dawn, we moved out once again. We stayed close to the Euphrates River all day long, and a few hours after the setting of the sun, we came to the town of al-Raqqa, where a good-sized stream joins the river. We could find no place in any of the khans and had to camp in the open air just within the walls of the town. We were to do that more than once in the course of our journey.

Three more days of traveling brought us to Aleppo. Aleppo I knew. Everyone in Baghdad knew Aleppo. It was the commercial center of Syria, and the town to which my uncle planned soon to send his seventh son. Caravan routes passed through not only to Baghdad, but also to Persia and India in the East, Asia Minor and Europe in the west, and Palestine and Egypt in the south.

I trailed through the city's huge bazaar, listening

as Jihha gossiped and bargained with shopkeepers. I kept both my ears wide open as he conducted wholesale business with traveling merchants right in the courtyards of khans and caravansaries, where the cloth, dried fruit, and licorice roots of Aleppo itself were traded for the wealth of the world. My chief was not a kind man or a good man, or a man whom others liked very much, but he was a shrewd man. It seemed to me he came out ahead in every transaction.

Perhaps he noticed how hard I listened. We stayed a week in Aleppo and then moved out toward Antioch. We camped one night on the way.

After the caravan halted I served his evening meal and then hurried away from him. I still had all the baggage to unpack. Jihha was so greedy he didn't even allow me to unload the animals before I served his food.

"Don't leave, boy," he called to me. "I want to speak to you."

The camels and donkey had been walking in heat and dust, their backs laden with heavy packs, for twelve hours, with only a brief respite at midday. They were more in need of their dinner than he was. "Rayyis," I protested, "Kaffi is crying for something to eat." Kaffi was the camel Jihha rode. "If I don't feed her soon, she'll get sick, perhaps even die."

He understood that. Kaffi was worth at least fifteen dinars, and if anything happened to her on the journey Gindar might hold Jihha responsible. "All right," he agreed grudgingly. "But come back as soon as you're done. Bring a bowl. You can have some soup."

I couldn't believe he was actually going to give me something to eat. I took care of the animals as quickly as I could, picked up a bowl from the small supply of copper vessels he carried in one of his packs, and joined him at the campfire.

"Sit down," he ordered.

I held out the bowl. He stared at it as if he hadn't the remotest notion of the use to which such an object was put. Then he lifted the pot off the fire and poured just enough soup in my bowl to cover the design on the bottom and not one drop more. I drank it quickly. I would have enjoyed it more with some bread, but if Jihha knew I had a little food of my own, I was sure he'd never give me another morsel.

"You made a mistake last week," he said.

"I made a lot of mistakes last week," I replied.

He actually smiled. I thought his cheeks might split from the effort. "I'm talking about the baby camel. He belonged to the son of Selim the One-Eared."

"Oh?"

"You should have come to me with the camel. I would've seen to it that you got the reward you deserved for returning it. Selim's rich as the caliph. He didn't earn his money honestly, I can tell you that. He's cheated me more than once."

"You would've seen to it that *I* got a reward?" I

made no effort to keep the irony out of my voice. Let him beat me if he wanted. Since the few lashes I had felt from him always stopped short of doing any real damage, I wasn't going to let their possibility crush me.

But Jihha didn't seem angry at me for speaking out. "Handing that camel over to Gindar did no one any good," he said in a reasonable tone.

"Except Selim the One-Eared's son, who shouldn't have to pay again for what's already his," I pointed out.

"It would've been a lesson to him. The sooner he learns that carelessness is expensive, the better off he'll be. He knows nothing about business, and neither do you." He glanced at me fleetingly, out of the corner of his eye.

"My father's a merchant," I protested, stung.

"In a very small way," Jihha reminded me. "Else you wouldn't be traveling caravan as my servant."

What he said was true. I looked up at him. "Teach me," I said.

"Teach you so that you can leave me?" he retorted sharply.

I smiled a little. "I'm not much of a servant."

"You're improving." He picked up his soup bowl and poured the liquid into his mouth. It was several seconds before he could speak again. "But I have no illusions. I know you'll leave me anyway, when we get to Tyre, if you last even that long."

I didn't deny it. "In Tyre you'll find a better servant than I could ever be." I was actually consoling him. The fire danced before us, and I stared into it as I spoke. All around us the ground was sprinkled with other fires that matched the fires in the star-studded sky. The warm smell and soft murmuring voices of beasts flowed about us, and in the distance I could hear a single voice, singing. For the first time in over a week I'd had almost enough to eat. I felt warm, drowsy, comfortable. I felt as if Jihha were almost my friend.

The evening must have been working on him in the same way. "There's more to you than meets the eye, Nasir," he said. It was the first time he'd spoken my name. I thought he'd forgotten it. "Obviously, you're poor, or you wouldn't have consented to travel as my servant. On the other hand, you speak like an educated man, you can read, and I daresay, write, and you had none of the skills a poor boy ought to possess. You couldn't saddle an animal, you couldn't fasten a pack. All you could manage those first couple of days was a little cooking. But you learned fast. Very fast." He uttered a sound that fell halfway between a cough and a laugh. "I know you watch me and listen to me. If you learn buying and selling as fast as you learned the knowledge of the trail, you'll drive the rest of us out of business in a month's time."

"I don't want to drive anyone out of business," I said. "In all the great stretch of land from the Persian

67

Gulf to the Mediterranean Sea, there must be enough goods for me to trade without taking food out of anyone else's mouth."

"You know nothing, boy," Jihha responded derisively. "There are only so many people and so many goods and so much money."

I leaned forward. I wanted to be sure he understood me. I had been thinking about the matter for a long time, for more than a year, ever since Hassan had visited our house before departing for Alexandria. It was then that the vague dreams with which I'd always filled my mind before I fell asleep began to take more definite forms. Fantasies had turned into plans. "There isn't a woman in Baghdad who doesn't have a bottle of rosewater to use when she wants to make sure her body gives off a pleasant odor," I said.

Jihha nodded. "Of course. Rosewater is a very good item. But don't think of rosewater. Selim the One-Eared has cornered the market in Damascus. The pressers sell only to him. He told them he'd slit their throats if they sold to anyone else, and they believe him. You've never seen Selim the One-Eared. He's twice as tall as his son, and his son stretches higher than Gindar. However," Jihha added thoughtfully, "sending his son to Damascus instead of going himself this time was a mistake. The son is stupid. Maybe rosewater isn't such a bad idea after all. If my son had lived, he'd have danced circles around the son of Selim the One-Eared."

"Oh, be quiet and listen to me," I cried impatiently. "You haven't given me a chance to make my point." Then it struck me that I was speaking to my employer, my violent-tempered employer, as if I were his equal. "Pardon my words, O rayyis," I added hastily. "My great joy at my chief's benevolence in deigning to carry on a conversation with me has perhaps overcome my manners."

But Jihha merely grunted. I took his "Hmm" as a signal to continue. "The rosewater is only an example. Once upon a time there was no such thing as rosewater. And then somewhere someone got the idea of capturing the scent of roses, so that women as well as flowers could give off sweet odors. From the day Allah created the world until that moment, women had lived perfectly well without rosewater. But if you told them that now, they wouldn't believe you. Rosewater has become a necessity. The poorest woman buys at least a small vial of it to use on her wedding day. Rich women bathe in it."

Jihha nodded slowly. "What you say is true, boy. Somewhere in there, back at the beginning, fortunes were made. But I still don't understand what good that'll do you."

"I'm talking about another rosewater," I said. "Don't you see? There has to be something else, some other item just lying around waiting to be seized upon by a clever merchant who by presenting it properly will convince everyone that it's a necessity. That merchant will be me!"

"I don't think there are any flowers left," Jihha responded gloomily. "They've all been made into perfumes already."

"Oh, no," I cried, forgetting again to whom I was speaking. "You're still missing the point. I don't want to sell something like rosewater. I want to find something new, something that goes into an empty space."

"But what could that be?" Jihha asked. "There are no empty spaces. Everything human beings need or want already exists."

"Do you really believe," I asked him quietly, "that nothing new waits for us? Do you really believe that?"

Jihha stared at me, his eyes wide with wonder. It was probably the first time since he'd grown up that his grease-encrusted brain had been penetrated by an idea that was something more than a repetition of a notion he'd thought about five hundred times before.

His eyes didn't hold mine for more than a second or two. Jihha wasn't comfortable with direct glances. He turned his gaze to the fire and stared into it without speaking. I didn't say anything either. I had to give him time to digest a new idea. But digest it he would, for his mind, if not original, was exceedingly shrewd.

When he spoke again, it was with brisk matter-of-factness. "Well, lad," he said, "when you come upon such an item, I hope you'll allow me to back you. You'll need capital. I can supply it, and we can share in the profits. That'll be a good laugh on Selim the One-Eared."

I wasn't surprised to hear him say that. True, I was only his servant, but if Jihha had sensed he could make money off a thief or an assassin, he wouldn't have hesitated to enter into an arrangement with him. But like the thief or assassin, I'd be on my guard. I was sure he'd cheated Selim the One-Eared as often as Selim the One-Eared had cheated him. I'd find a way to insure that he wouldn't cheat me. However, all I said out loud was, "Thank you, my chief. After we reach the coast, I'll remember this conversation."

"And I'll remember it, too," said Jihha.

We spoke together many evenings after that. During the day I was only his servant, and he screamed at me and cursed me with every other breath. But I followed him faithfully as he went about his business, and in the dark, especially while we were traveling, we forgot all that and became not exactly equals, not exactly friends, but something like that—teacher and pupil, perhaps. He told me the best spot in a bazaar to locate a stall. He told me how to lay out goods so that they showed to advantage. He told me where and when to shop to acquire what I needed at the cheapest prices. He explained to me in detail the elaborate ritual of bargaining, which I knew in part from the buyer's end. It was a game I'd always enjoyed, though I'd rarely been allowed to play, since my mother enjoyed it too and did most of the shopping for our family. The merchant's side wasn't hard, not really. It just required a certain amount of willpower. The merchant knew what an item had cost him. He had to figure not only the cash he'd expended to obtain it, but also the expense he'd been put to get and then to sell it. To that he added a reasonable margin of profit. That was the lowest price at which he dared to sell the item. He had that figure in his head, and he knew he couldn't go below it. It was better for him not to sell the thing, to keep it until another day, than to sell it below that previously determined figure.

Usually. There were exceptions, and Jihha taught me all about them too. If you had overbought on vests and winter was nearly over, it was better to sell them cheap than to go to the bother and expense of storing them over the summer. The loss would be less than the cost of holding onto them. Sensing when the moment had come at which to let go—that, said Jihha, was an art and an instinct. No one could teach it to you. "But," he added drily, "I don't doubt you possess it."

As my father didn't, which was one reason he'd never earned more than a bare living. My father didn't have the courage trading required either. "You see," Jihha explained, "sometimes you have to take a risk. It's your instinct that tells you when to do that too. Take those vests I was talking about. At a bazaar in a little village late in the summer you come across an old woman with a hundred of them to sell. She's been making them for years. She's selling them very cheap.

Should you buy them? If we have a cold winter, you'll make a good profit. If the winter's mild, you're stuck with them. You weigh all the factors. The last three winters have been mild. We seem about due for a cold one. On the other hand, the fortune-teller with whom you chatted in the suq said we're in a cycle of seven warm winters to be followed by seven cold ones. But then again, how much does the fortune-teller really know? Is he a truly competent fortune-teller, or just a charlatan? These are the things you have to consider, all very quickly, before deciding whether or not to take the risk. But sometimes you do. Sometimes you must. You'll never make a decent living unless you're willing, sometimes, to take a risk."

As my father wasn't. As he thought he couldn't afford to be. As he should have been—for truly, he didn't have much to lose.

And then I realized that at last my father had taken a risk. He'd taken a risk on me.

Jihha was still talking. "That's why I'm willing to back you when you decide what it is you want to buy and then sell to fill up the empty space," he said. "That and my desire to beat out old Selim. Backing you will be a risk, but I've always known when to take a risk, and when not to. Oh, naturally, I've made a few mistakes, but not many. I wouldn't be where I am today if I had."

I learned a great deal from Jihha. I learned so much that it was worth every cross word, every curse,

73

to have served him on those journeyings across the desert, and during all those weeks in the bazaars and suqs of Aleppo, Antioch, Ladhiqiyah, Beirut, and Damascus. I became convinced that the product I would sell was growing quiet and unnoticed somewhere in a wilderness or oasis or along the banks of a tiny stream. It was the sweet attar of a hidden flower, or the soothing drug or unguent from a secret plant. Meanwhile, I learned what I could about the business of buying and selling perfumes and medicinal herbs, asking, listening, watching everywhere we went.

The caravan broke up in Damascus. A few of us, including Jihha and myself, accompanied Gindar and Abu Sinan west to the coastal city of Tyre. Summer was nearly gone by the time we got there. As Gindar had predicted the night I'd returned the baby camel, the flab on my arms had turned to muscle. The weight on my hips had disappeared. My skin was dark. And my head was full of all that I'd learned on the way.

Before the remnants of the caravan dispersed, I sought out Gindar. I knew he wouldn't remain long in Tyre. In a week's time, or less, he'd be traveling across the desert again, if not back to Baghdad, then south through the Arabian peninsula to some distant city unreachable from the coast by any means except the back of a camel.

I found him in his room in the caravansary with Abu Sinan, collecting the money still owed him by the last of the travelers, who'd paid him half prior to departing and now owed him the other half upon their safe arrival. I waited until his business with the others was done, and then I stepped forward.

"Why are you here, Nasir?" he asked when he saw me. "You don't owe me anything. Between the return of the baby camel, and the way you kept Jihha too occupied to make trouble for anyone else, I should pay you for having traveled with us."

"Surely," I replied, "I owe you my thanks. Everything you said would happen has happened. I'm strong. I'm wiry. I don't know if I'm wise, but Jihha and my own eyes have certainly taught me things I'd never before even guessed at."

Gindar nodded. "You're a man now, my friend." He smiled a little, and added very softly, "Insofar as that's possible."

My hand went to my breast and pulled the two edges of my jubba tightly together. I didn't know what to say. To tell the truth, after twelve weeks among men only, after twelve weeks without ever looking at my own self, I'd almost forgotten I was a woman. That doesn't mean I thought of myself as a man. I was only me, Nasir, servant and student of the merchant Jihha.

I glanced at Abu Sinan. Had he heard what Gindar had said? Apparently, for he nodded slightly. What Gindar knew, Abu Sinan knew.

"Your secret's safe, my friend," Gindar said. "No one would guess now. A season's travel has taken care of that."

"But if you knew," I whispered, "why did you let me come?"

Gindar shrugged. "My mother's a black woman," he said. "She was a slave stolen from a tribe that lives south of the Sahara. My father was an Arab trader whose name she's forgotten and I never knew. I've made my way in the world by my wits and my strength and my skills. I know the desert like the palm of my hand, and men such as my father must pay me very well for the benefit of that knowledge. Very well."

"Yes," I agreed. "Very well indeed. Five dinars supports my father's entire house for weeks."

"I'm rich," he said. "I bought my mother out of slavery long ago. I could buy a thousand others like her. But I don't. I don't spend all my substance freeing her people."

The cheerfulness that usually graced his face was gone. He looked so stricken as he said those words that my heart went out to him. "Surely Allah requires no such sacrifice from you." I tried to comfort him.

"It's not a matter of what Allah requires of me," he said. "It's a matter of what I require of myself." His smile was grim. "You're running away from some kind of slavery, aren't you?" I opened my mouth to explain, but he held up his hand. "I don't need to know what it is—a cruel father, a distasteful marriage, an importunate master. I don't want to know. On my caravan, I don't ask questions. I told you that once before. It's enough for me to realize I didn't send you back to a slave's existence."

"I have more to thank you for than I dreamed." There was nothing else I could say.

He rose and held out his hand. I took it, grasping it firmly in mine. "Your hand is small, friend Nasir," he said. "But it's hard and strong. No one will know until you choose to let them know." He shook mine, hard. "And that's a thing you'll do when you yourself are satisfied with whoever you are—or have become. You know you can trust me."

"I never doubted it," I replied quietly. "Today I have less reason to doubt it than ever."

He nodded. "If, at any time, you need a message, or goods, or money carried to Baghdad, I'll do it. I'm usually in Tyre a couple of times a year. Whatever you give me to be delivered will be delivered just as you handed it to me. Whatever secret you entrust to me won't go a jot beyond my ears."

"Thank you, Cindar. I'll remember that."

"There's nothing to add, then," he said, smiling, "except good luck. Peace be with you, Nasir, my friend."

"And with you, peace, Rayyis Gindar," I returned. Then I picked up my bundle, straightened my shoulders, lifted my chin, and marched out of the caravansary like a soldier.

Jihha had gone to the bathhouse to wash the dust of the long journey from his flesh. He had a lot of flesh to wash. It would take him a long time. He'd suggested that I accompany him, but I had told him I couldn't let Gindar depart without making a proper farewell.

I'd told Jihha I'd wait for him in the khan. But I didn't. I had questioned him closely about the town and its surroundings. When I left the caravansary, I made my way through city streets to the widest gate in the city wall. I walked swiftly across a flat plain and then turned and headed toward the sea. There, on a deserted strip of beach, I took off all my clothes and bathed myself.

I'd never before washed myself anywhere but in the large wooden tub my mother placed in our court-yard or our room. I'd certainly never bathed in the sea. I'd never even seen the sea. But as soon as I laid eyes upon it, I couldn't wait until I was in it. The sight, the sound, the smell of it were like the sight and sound and smell of home. It seemed to me that I belonged in it. And when the bitter taste of salt filled my mouth, when its sharpness stung my eyes, when clear blue-greenness lapped over my head, I knew that the sea felt like home, too. Every one of my senses was filled with delight at the very same moment. Truly, if nothing more happened to me on my journey than this experience of wave and whitecap, I would be satisfied. At least, that's how I felt at the moment.

I came out of the water and stood dripping on the empty beach, warm sand between my toes, warm sun beating on my back, my body tingling clean. Hastily, I dried myself. I threw on my clothes and hurried back toward the town. Now I was ready. I was ready for whatever fate awaited me behind the high white walls of Tyre.

Part 2

MAHMUD, SON OF OMAR, the Wali of
Tyre, called al-Katib, his secretary, to his bedside
one night. "I cannot sleep," he said.

"Perhaps your servant made a mistake," the
secretary replied. "You must have meant to send
for the palace physician, who could prescribe a
sleeping draught for you."

"There's been no mistake," said Mahmud.
"I sent for you because it's you I want. I want
you to write down the words I say to you."

"My lord writes as fine a hand as I," the man
protested.

"If you record what I say, you become a wit-
ness to the fact that the words were indeed mine,"
Mahmud replied. "If my father returns from the
hunt one day and finds me gone from this place,

81

you will appear before him and tell him that you heard these words issue from my lips with your own ears. But before that day you will say nothing of this to anyone."

Al-Katib settled himself cross-legged on the carpet. He opened the little writing desk Prince Mahmud kept in his room and took out paper, quill pen, and ink. He sharpened the pen with a knife and dipped it in the bottle. "Proceed, *mawlana al-amir*," he said. "Proceed, my lord, the prince.

I, MAHMUD OF TYRE, speak these words. Let any human being upon whose ears they fall learn from the errors of a foolish man who lacked sufficient wisdom to trust the promptings of his own heart.

My father is Wali of Tyre. He governs the city and all the lands about it by the grace and authority of the mighty Fatimid Caliph who rules his vast domain from his new capital, Cairo, in Egypt.

My tale begins on a day in the spring, a hot day, much too hot a day for so early in the season. I had spent the morning with my father, listening to the petitions of those seeking redress of grievances or rewards for some service, real or imagined. After each petition, my father conferred with me and his vizier and then rendered his judgement or decision. In spite of the servants ceaselessly waving fans, the heat pressed upon me. I forced my face to wear the calm, impenetrable, yet concerned expression that is expected of the prince, but it cost me greater effort than usual.

Recently, an unaccustomed restlessness had seized me. My duties as prince and probable future Wali of Tyre no longer absorbed me as once they had. My companionship with the young men of the city no longer satisfied me. My father said that it was time for me to marry, but the prospect afforded me no delight. I thought I was content with the slave girls I called for whenever the mood struck me. I did not need a wife, who would intrude upon my studies, my work, my recreations—at least, not yet. But if it was not a wife I wanted, it seemed I wanted something, something neither I nor anyone else could name.

By the time we had heard the last petitioner, the sweat under my arms had stained my shirt and my head ached with heat and boredom. I rose from the cushion-strewn rug on which I was sitting, just to the right of and a little bit below my father. I bowed before him. "My father," I said, "it's hotter today than it's been since last summer. I'm going to bathe."

"Not here," my father suggested. "Not in the palace. Go to the public bath. You'll meet your friends there; you'll relax and enjoy yourself."

"I have no friends," I retorted. "Only hangers-on, sycophants, people who want something from me."

"People in our position can't expect anything else," my father replied quietly.

"Doesn't that upset you?" I asked.

He shrugged. "I'm used to it. Forewarned is forearmed. And what am I to do on that account? Avoid all human contact? That's what you're starting to do. You're turning into a pompous old man, Mahmud, and you're only twenty-two years old!"

"I'm sorry, my father," I returned stiffly. "We're all different. Much as I respect you, I cannot emulate you in everything." My father certainly enjoyed himself, but most of the things that gave him pleasure meant nothing to me at all. A harem full of slaves, endless banquets, elaborate hunting parties—all of these seemed to me to be far more trouble than they were worth, and absurdly expensive too.

"Amin and Uthman are your good friends," my father urged. "Go to the bathhouse with them."

"Very well, mawlana al-wali," I replied formally, "if that is your will."

"In the name of the Prophet," my father cried in exasperation, "do you think it really matters to me whether you bathe with your friends or bathe alone? I just can't stand the sight of you moping around in corners on such a hot day."

That meant, "Get out of here." I left for the bathhouse, followed at a discreet distance by the two servants who accompanied me wherever I went. I would meet Amin and Uthman, my two closest companions, as my father had urged.

My companions. But were they my friends? How many times had I lent Amin money? Once a week, at least, for as long as I had known him. Not that he ever asked for it in so many words. When Uthman suggested a game of backgammon at the gaming house, Amin would laugh and say, "Certainly, my friend, if you're willing to play for sesame seeds." Then I would advance him the money. I would never ask for it back, and he would never offer it.

Uthman had no need of my money. His father, a dealer in gold and precious gems, was probably richer than mine. Abu Uthman had recently sold my father a heavy, jewel-encrusted bracelet for the Nubian princess he had recently married. Of course, my stepmother, the first wife, when she saw the Nubian's gift, demanded something even more spectacular for herself. Abu Uthman obligingly supplied a gold collar set with forty emeralds. It suited my stepmother, an Egyptian, perfectly, and she was actually quite pleasant to the Nubian for nearly three weeks. It struck me suddenly that Uthman never gave Amin money. I was the only one of whom that was expected.

When I greeted them at the bathhouse entrance, where they were waiting for me, I did so with no more than a nod.

"What's the matter, mawlana?" Amin teased. "Has the heat melted your tongue?"

Amin amused me. That is why, in spite of my suspicions, I could not forgo his company. "It's been a long morning," I replied. "My father and I must have listened to two hundred petitioners. Everyone wants something from me. I feel as if a thousand tiny fish are eating me up."

Uthman glanced at Amin. Amin merely lifted his eyebrows and said nothing. "Come, my prince," Uthman said. "I guarantee you, after an afternoon in the bathhouse, you'll feel much better."

Uthman was right, of course. We entered the bathhouse and disrobed. Over our bodies we poured the heated water that flowed into stone basins flush with the tiled floor. Then we covered ourselves and lay down on pallets to gossip and joke while the sweat rolled off us. By the time the attendants brought us sherbet and sweetmeats, my headache had left me, my muscles were relaxed, and the air around me actually seemed cool and refreshing, as even the hot desert wind would after the steaming water. I was at my ease, and too drained of energy to feel anger any longer, or even annoyance.

"Listen," Amin said when we were back in the dressing room, where my servants assisted the three of us in putting on our clothes, "we have a treat for you. You might call it a gift."

I smiled a little. "What kind of gift can you give me, Amin?" I asked. "You never have enough cash to buy an apple from a street vendor." Uthman often scolded Amin for his empty money belt. This was the first time I had ever mentioned the subject.

Amin did not take offense. "This gift costs me nothing," he said. "Yet it's the most valuable gift I can give you."

"Where is it?"

"Waiting for us in a shop in the Sharie al-Khalifa." That was the street we often strolled, as did most of the other young men of Amin's and Uthman's class—the sons of the large landowners, shipbuilders, and merchants who formed the aristocracy of Tyre. Whatever the gift was, I wondered in what way I would eventually be expected to pay for it.

But the bath had put me in charity with my friends once again. I pushed the petty notion from my mind and led the way out of the bathhouse. We walked along the quay toward Sharie al-Khalifa, for even on the hottest day a breeze blew in from the harbor, making the docks the pleasantest place in town.

The street we sought was a short stroll inland from the quay. Amin hurried ahead; Uthman and I followed dutifully. We came to the best suq in Tyre, the one that featured the highest-quality merchandise at the most expensive prices. In the suq we passed the jewelry stall of Abu Uthman; a few paces beyond it was a large, airy, well-arranged shop featuring unguents, medicines, and perfumes. I had never seen it before. The last time I had bothered to notice, I thought a cloth merchant had occupied the space.

A slight, remarkably good-looking young man was pointing out an herb-filled earthenware jar to a customer. "Look," said Amin with a wave of his hand. "There's my gift."

"Your gift?" What made Amin think I was in need of either medicine or scents?

"A friend," Amin replied simply. "Could there be a better gift?"

I smiled. "No, Amin, if a friend he truly proves to be. But I don't think the gift of friendship is something one man can give on behalf of another. He can only give it for himself."

Amin smiled too. "You'll see, my prince," he said. "You'll see."

We entered the shop and watched while the young man weighed out herbs for the customer and accepted some coins in payment. The customer departed, and Amin called out, "Nasir! Alsalamu alaykum."

"And with you, peace," the young man called Nasir replied. His black eyes sparkled in his smooth, merry face. He was dressed in colors as bright as a woman would wear. His silk caftan was heavily embroidered at the sleeves and the bottom of the skirt. A few unruly black curls escaped from beneath his purple silk turban. He smiled, and it was a smile of such melting sweetness that he could have been dressed in rags for all I cared.

"Here's the guest I promised you," Amin said. "Here's our lord the prince Mahmud, son of the Wali of Tyre."

Nasir bowed low. "Peace be with you, mawlana al-amir," he said.

I nodded my head. "And to you, peace," I replied. "Please, please, all of you, do me the honor of seating yourselves."

"The honor is ours, mawlana," Nasir murmured. His tone, his manner, were correct and respectful, but not obsequious. He snapped his fingers. A servant appeared from the rear of the shop, carrying pillows. After we had seated ourselves, he disappeared, returning later with sherbet and sweetmeats.

"Well, Nasir," I said, "how did it happen that a perfectly respectable shopkeeper like yourself came to be acquainted with these two reprobates? I'm stuck with them. We grew up together. But you're new in town. You can choose your friends."

Amin did not give Nasir a chance to reply. "He's Jihha's new partner. That makes him as much a reprobate as the rest of us."

Uthman prided himself on his dignity. "Speak for yourself, Amin," he reproved.

"Who in the name of heaven is Jihha?" I asked.

"You know, that fat, foul-mouthed merchant who turns up here in Tyre at least once a year," Amin replied. "He does a lot of business with Abu Uthman."

"My father never had a thing to do with Jihha," Uthman protested angrily. "My father's honesty is a byword throughout the Caliphate. What could he possibly have to do with a character as questionable as Jihha?"

"Plenty, this year," Amin retorted. "Plenty, since Nasir's become Jihha's partner."

So far Nasir had not said a word. It wasn't easy to squelch Amin long enough to squeeze in a remark, but I held up my hand, signaling him to be quiet. "What miracles have you wrought, Nasir, to turn this apparent scoundrel, Jihha, into such a model of propriety that even the sainted Abu Uthman will deal with him?"

Nasir smiled and shrugged. His voice, when he spoke, was pleasant and light. "I'm afraid Jihha is still a scoundrel," he said, "but he's been good to me. And I watch him very closely. We're making so much money he doesn't really need to do anything dishonest."

Nasir looked so young that it was obvious he was just starting out in business. How had he gotten so rich so quickly? "Your father is a man of wealth?" I queried.

"Nasir is a man of genius," Amin interjected.

"No, no," Nasir protested quickly. "I'm not. And my father isn't rich either. I've been lucky, that's all. Allah has blessed me."

"Tell me about it," I suggested. Nasir's eyes glanced first at Uthman and then at Amin. They nodded slightly. A request from me, was, after all, an order, no matter how I phrased it.

"My father's a merchant," Nasir explained, "but he never prospered. His little shop couldn't support me, too. I had to make my own way. A caravan passed by on its way to the coast. I decided to join it and seek my fortune here."

"Passed by where?" I asked.

Nasir's expression was puzzled.

"Where are you from?" I clarified my question with another.

"Oh, a little town," he said. "A tiny little town far from the sea. You've never heard of it."

I still wanted to know its name. However, I had no opportunity to say so. Nasir went right on telling his story.

"That was my first piece of luck—the caravan. For that's where I met Jihha. It seems he has no sons, at least not living, or daughters, or, so far as I can tell, even a wife. He sort of . . . well, he sort of adopted me."

"Humph," snorted Uthman. "I somehow can't believe that Jihha has ever done anything out of the goodness of his heart. He must have recognized your genius immediately."

"Don't be ridiculous, Uthman," Nasir responded sharply. "I'm not a genius. I wish you and Amin would stop referring to me by that term. It's embarrassing." He turned to me with a smile. "Our lord the prince will never embarrass me in such a way."

"I can't say, my friend," I replied. "So far you're in no danger. I've had no evidence of your genius."

Nasir's smile was wide, brilliant, open. I felt pleasure simply in seeing it. "I'm safe," he said. "You never will."

Now it was Amin's turn to snort. "To make a long story short," he said, "Nasir trades in medicinal herbs, among other things. No one here thought anything about those powders wise women out in the country use to stop bleeding and clear stuffed heads. It took a stranger to realize that those particular cures don't exist in other places and to make a profit out of them. Now tell me he's not a genius!"

Uthman shook his head. "Those herbs, berries, roots—whatever they are—have been around here all these years and we paid no attention. Jihha backed Nasir, but the discoveries were all his. Imagine poking into dusty corners and turning up gold."

"Gold that no one else was even aware of," Amin added. "Such an accomplishment couldn't be kept secret. It's spoken of in every shop in the bazaar. And of course he's branched out. He's into lots of things now."

I looked at Nasir with respect. "Well, I won't call you a genius since you don't like the term," I said, "but you must admit you're very clever."

However, he would not grant even that. "Lucky, mawlana, lucky. The herbs are commonplace to you— like weeds. You wouldn't realize how remarkable they appear to someone who comes from a place where nothing like them grows."

"Jihha is from such a place," Uthman pointed out. "Baghdad, I believe."

"Or perhaps Aleppo," Nasir said. "I'm not sure."

"Wherever." Uthman waved his hand dismissively. "The point is that until you came along, Jihha never had the wit to realize that the herbs were important, any more than did any of the hordes of traders from other places who descend upon this city. It never occurred to them to look for gold where no one else had ever found it."

"There are countless herbs in our fields worth looking into, Nasir," I said. "You'll be with us a long time. I'm glad of that."

He bowed his head briefly. "Thank you, mawlana," he said. "I have six sisters. I have to provide for each of them. I need to earn a lot. I want them to have very good husbands."

"You're the only son?"

"Hmm . . . yes. The only kind of son my father will ever have."

"Are you the eldest?"

"No, I'm the fourth."

I laughed. "What rejoicing there must have been the day you were born. In an instant the name of your father changed from Abu al-Banat to Abu Nasir. He must bless your name with every breath he takes."

"My father loves me," he said. His voice was so low I had to lean forward to hear him. "He loves my sisters too."

"Of course, of course," I replied. "But what are six daughters, or even twelve daughters, compared to one son?"

His glance locked mine. "Daughters can do very well," he said. There was a surprising undertone of anger in his voice.

"Is that what your father says?" I asked.

Suddenly he grinned again. The storm was over, passing as suddenly as it had come. "I don't know. I never asked him. I think, if you'll pardon me, mawlana, that this is a foolish conversation."

"You're right," I agreed. "Come. Let's play backgammon. We'll see how lucky you really are, Nasir, and how clever."

He was both. He beat all of us at backgammon on that very first day. And I was glad of him, from that very first day. Before, if I played with Uthman, I was distracted by Amin's endless stream of chatter. And if I played with Amin, I had to listen to Uthman's whispered advice on strategy. He was usually wrong, but invariably withdrew into hurt silence if I did not follow his suggestions. And if I watched Uthman and Amin play with each other, I was always bored, because they played so badly. Now there were four of us. We could all play at the same time. From that first day on, I manipulated our games so that I played most often with Nasir. At last I had found a backgammon opponent worthy of me.

And a friend worthy of me too. I loved Amin and

Uthman, but my love for them was always darkened by my belief that their love for me was tainted by self-interest. I never had to worry about that with Nasir. He wanted nothing from me, he needed nothing from me, except my friendship.

But was I worthy of him? In those days I never thought to ask that question.

Nasir worked hard. He did not have the leisure Amin, Uthman, or even I enjoyed. He was too busy in his shop to join us at the bath or the gaming house, too busy to take whole days from his trade to hunt with us or play polo, and only on rare occasions could he ride. Usually, the most he could spare us on a regular basis were a few hours in the late afternoon, when we would meet at his shop or our favorite gaming house. Although he worked hard and joined us late, he never seemed weary or cross. So sharp was his wit, so clever his tongue, so warm his smile, that the time he was with us was the best time of the day.

After we dined, Uthman and Amin often spent the later part of the evening with entertainers, slaves who had been trained to sing and dance in Damascus. I did not. It was not seemly for the prince to appear in such company, and besides I had all that I required of that sort of thing among the slave girls of the palace. Nasir never went either. Night after night Amin urged him to come along. Always he refused.

"Nasir, what kind of man are you?" Amin cried in annoyance one evening. "You don't hunt with us, you don't go to the bath with us, and you don't look for girls with us."

Uthman shook Amin by the shoulder. "Nasir doesn't have to explain himself. If he lacks our bad habits, the more credit to him."

"Hunting and bathing aren't bad habits." Amin's tone was petulant.

"I don't mind explaining myself to my friends," Nasir said calmly. "I don't hunt because I don't know how. I come from a poor family, remember? We hadn't the money to indulge ourselves in aristocratic pastimes."

"You have the money now," Amin said.

"Yes, but not the time to learn. I do need exercise, though. I'm getting fat, like Jihha." He patted his stomach briskly. It did not look any rounder to me than it had the day I had first met him. "Later, perhaps, when I've got everything under control, I'll hire a hunting tutor." Nasir laughed. "As for bathing, do I emit a foul odor?"

"You chose to misunderstand me," Amin interrupted. "I'm not saying you don't bathe. I'm saying you don't bathe with us."

"For me bathing is simply a matter of keeping clean," he explained apologetically. "You know that when you go to the bathhouse you spend almost the whole day there. I just don't have the time to turn washing into a social occasion. Amin, I hope that doesn't offend you. Your friendship is precious to me."

Perhaps Amin was jealous of the fondness that Uthman and I had conceived for Nasir. Whatever the reason, he was in no mood that night to let our friend off easily. "What about the girls?" he asked directly.

"Mahmud doesn't go to see them either," Nasir replied, his eyes holding Amin's.

"Mahmud doesn't need to. We do."

"Every man is different," Uthman said in a soothing voice.

"Not in that respect," Amin said. "Not if he's a man."

But Nasir was not to be baited. He merely smiled. "Perhaps, then, in that respect, I'm not a man," he said. "If you wish to avoid my company on that account, so be it."

"Some men are more fastidious than others." Uthman was still trying to explain.

"Are you suggesting that we frequent places that aren't clean?" Amin asked indignantly.

I stood up. "This conversation has passed the bounds of propriety," I said. "Amin, be on your way. Go wherever it is you have to go. Uthman, you go with him, since he appears to be incapable of taking three steps without company. Nasir complains of a lack of exercise. He and I will walk."

And so we did. It became a habit. After dinner, Uthman and Amin would go about their own business, and Nasir and I would walk along the quay. Amin grew increasingly morose and increasingly acid in the remarks he addressed to Nasir, but he really could do nothing about the deepening companionship between Nasir and me. Amin's credit, financial and social, depended heavily on the fact that he was my friend, and so it was important to him to remain on good terms with me, regardless of what I chose to do.

Night after night Nasir and I walked next to the water, enveloped by the warm black night. The only sounds that reached us were the wavelets slapping gently against the sides of the boats lying at anchor in the harbor and the creaking of their planks and rigging. If we passed a khan frequented by sailors, we heard shouts of laughter or raucous singing, but it seemed to be coming from a great distance. The stars shone; and sometimes the moon. Later, when the rainy season came, and the sky was frequently overcast, we picked our way by the light of the lanterns carried by my servants, one walking twenty paces in front of us, the other twenty paces behind. On such nights it seemed to me that Nasir and I were the only two people fully alive in the whole world.

We talked about everything. He knew little of science or philosophy. I had read widely in both areas, and he drank in what I told him with the eagerness of a thirsty man swallowing water in the desert. He knew as many tales of jinns and magic carpets as the story-teller who sat in the bazaar, and he entertained me with them for whole evenings at a time. We talked about politics and business. I told him how tedious and yet how fascinating I found it to learn to rule, and he revealed to me the intricacies of international trade.

He told me other things he said he had never revealed to another living human being. He told me what it was like to grow up poor and despised. He spoke particularly of a wealthy uncle who refused to help his brother, Nasir's father, in a practical way, but called on him daily to boast of his own triumphs. He mentioned a cousin, a man named Hassan, who had rejected the idea of marriage to one of Nasir's sisters with sneers and insults. That pain still rankled and was one of the main reasons, I was sure, for Nasir's passionate and energetic pursuit of money. But he never drew me into that pursuit. He never tried to sell me or any member of my family anything. Perhaps he had customers enough without us. But then, so did Abu Uthman, and that did not stop him from trading on his son's acquaintance with me. Nasir never tried to make use of me. He never tried to gain some kind of advantage from our friendship.

Walking, talking, and playing backgammon were not our only pastimes. Nasir would neither hunt nor play polo, but after a while he purchased a red mare and went riding with us. He rode well enough, though he never seemed to merge with his mount in the manner of a truly skilled horseman. That may have been because he had not ridden as a boy. His father had been too poor to keep a horse.

One day, when we were riding down a mountainside to the east of the city, Nasir's horse stumbled. Nasir fell off and rolled halfway down the hill. If he was not dead, I was sure he was at best marred for the rest of his life. When I discovered he had suffered nothing more than superficial bruises, I was so relieved I had to turn away so that Amin and Uthman could not see my tears.

Afterwards, we discovered that Nasir's horse had tripped because she had thrown a shoe. A rider more skilled than Nasir could perhaps have held his seat. He rode back to the city mounted behind me, his arms around my waist. I was in a cold sweat all the way home, thinking how close I had come to losing the best friend I had ever known—indeed, I thought, the only true friend I had. I would have been content if he never rode a horse again. Night walks were safer.

And more revealing, even in the dark. On those night walks I, like him, eventually spoke about things I had never mentioned to anyone else, not to Uthman, not to Amin, not to anyone. I told Nasir how much I had feared my father when I was a little boy; I told him how, although I was surrounded by people day and night, my soul always seemed as alone and as naked as it is at the moment of birth and death. And then one night, one black, starless night, I told him about the day my mother had died.

"I was nine," I began. "I was nine when my mother died. She had explained to me about the wonderful thing that was going to happen. I was going to have a little brother. She was sure it was a brother. She never even considered the possibility that it might be a girl. Of course, I had many half-brothers and sisters, but this new one was to be a prince, like me, because my mother was the princess. She was full of joy, and every day her joy increased. She spent hours playing games with me and telling me stories. We would have an even better time together, she said, after the new baby came, for then my father would join us, because he would be so happy that at last I had a brother.

"But joy did not survive the baby's birth. He was a little prince, as she had known he would be, and he died the day he was born. They took me to see her. She hugged me and kissed me and told me not to miss her, because she'd be watching over me from Paradise. Then she died too, and I did miss her, in spite of what she said. I've missed her ever since. I learned then that even your mother and your father cannot keep you safe from pain. I learned that they cannot always tell you the truth. I was too young for those lessons. They should have come later."

"Ah, mawlana," Nasir said softly, "you haven't really loved another human being since."

I had never thought of that, but I realized it was true. "How do you know so much, Nasir?" I asked.

"You just told me."

"I didn't tell you that."

"But you did."

In the darkness, I smiled. Nasir could not see my

smile. "Now you tell me something," I said. "Let's see if I can learn as much from as little."

He did not reply. "Come on, Nasir," I urged. "It's only fair." I reached out and grasped his upper arm tightly. I felt a shiver run through his muscles, as if in response to my touch, and I, as if in response to his, felt my hand tremble. Hastily, I pulled it away, as if I had grasped fire.

Nasir began to speak, slowly. "I've been luckier than you," he said quietly. "I have a mother who loves me very much, and a father who always had time to talk to me and teach me. Perhaps poverty has some compensations. I never realized that before. Money brings so many responsibilities. It takes so much time to be rich."

"Not for Uthman," I pointed out.

"Well," he said, "it does in the beginning. It does for me now."

"You never had close friends before," I interpreted. "You'd like to be able to spend more time with us."

His voice was so low I had to lean closer to him to hear his reply. "With you, mawlana," he said. "With you."

My blood surged with a sudden rush of joy. It was like nothing I had ever felt before. It washed away the melancholy that usually afflicted my spirits. He loved me. He loved me absolutely and without conditions. It did not matter what I said to him, or what I did or did not do for him. He loved me for me, and I loved him for him, and for what I was when I was with him—free, happy, and unconstrained. "You're my friend," I said. "I never had a true friend before."

"Nor I, my lord," he replied, "except for my sisters."

"Women can't be true friends," I said. "It isn't in their natures."

"That's not true." His voice was sharp. "My older sisters are too different from me to be my friends. They don't care about any of the things that matter to me. But the day will come when the youngest, little Darirah, will be my friend. I know it. And Zaynab could be my friend too, if she weren't so jealous of me."

"That's ridiculous, Nasir," I said. "Women are concerned with children and housekeeping and adorning their bodies. How can you possibly share anything with any of them? Little Darirah will never really grow up. Women are like children."

"As was your mother?" he countered instantly.

"I was a child when she died," I reminded him.

"And you've never been close to a woman since. Mawlana, you know nothing about them."

I was annoyed. "And you—you who won't go out with Uthman and Amin—you know?"

He did not get angry. It seemed as if I had known he would not. I could say anything to him. "My prince," he replied, "I admit freely to you what Amin suspects—I've never known a woman as a man knows a woman. But you know women only in that way, which means you don't know them at all!"

"All right, all right," I admitted with a laugh. "You have six sisters. Perhaps I have a dozen, but since I've never said more than two words to any of them at one time, it's possible that you know something I don't."

He laughed too, that warm, low, generous laugh that I had grown to anticipate with such pleasure. "It's possible," he said, "more possible than you can know."

"What do you mean?" I countered.

"Nothing."

"Don't talk in riddles. There should be no secrets between us."

"There has to be."

"Nasir, what do you mean?"

"I'll tell you." He paused.

"Go ahead. Tell me."

"Someday."

I reached out to seize him again, but he must have sensed what I was about to do. He laughed again and began to run. I chased after him. He was not so much out of condition as he had claimed to be some months before. In fact he was very fast. In a moment he had passed the servant who walked in front of us.

I was faster, and I knew the quayside better than he. Soon he would come to the wooden balustrade separating the dock from the lagoon, and there he would have to pause. I rushed headlong toward it and reached it a moment after he did. He did not know which way to turn. I put my hands flat against the wall on either side of him, trapping him in place. We were both breathless from the run. I was flushed, and from his rapid, heavy breathing, I guessed that he was too. "Tell me," I said. "Come on, Nasir, tell me your secret."

"There's no secret, prince," he said softly. "Truly my prince there is no secret."

We were very close. I could feel the heat rising from his body as it rose in mine. Quickly I pulled my hands away from the wall. I moved back several steps. "You have nothing to tell me?" I asked. "Nothing to reveal to me?"

"No, mawlana." Again his voice was so low I had to strain to hear it.

It seemed to me unwise to remain with him any longer. I clenched my fists and turned my back to him. In a moment I had recovered my usual manner, Prince Mahmud's manner. "Good night, Nasir," I said. "One of my servants will light your way home. Tomorrow I won't see you. An embassy from Alexandria arrived today, and tomorrow night there's a state dinner for them. Perhaps we'll meet at the shop the day after."

"Yes, mawlana al-amir." Nasir's voice was cool too, and formal.

I turned away and walked back to my servants. I sent Abdullah with Nasir, and accompanied by Faris, I returned to the palace. Once home again, I called for the slave girl who pleased me most. I had to do something to ease my confusion. But she did not help. I could not get Nasir out of my head. If he felt as I felt, which I suspected he did, what was he doing at this very moment? What was he thinking about? What was he imagining himself to be?

I could not get him out of my head that night, or the next day either. Certainly, since I had known him, since we had begun the night walks in which at last I had been able to unburden my soul to another human being, I had become a more cheerful man. My father had noticed it, all his advisers had noticed it. The air of resignation that I had used to wear was gone. I was actually quite willing to do what I had to do because I knew a treat and a pleasure waited for me at the end of the day—the company of one with whom I did not have to be anyone but myself.

I still felt absurdly happy, perhaps even more so than I had before. But now I was also worried. The next day I moved about the palace so preoccupied by my own thoughts that I bumped into furniture. My father's vizier had to speak to me three times to get my attention. At least so he told me, with some asperity. Since I did not hear him the first two times, I would not otherwise have known.

I could not join my friends that night because of the state dinner for the Alexandrian embassy. The celebration continued all night. After ten, I stopped counting the courses. Later, the slaves danced. Rina, my favorite, danced the most sinuously of all. But I did not call for her. I let her go, as was polite, to one of the guests. I did not want her anyway. As I sat watching her graceful brown body move under the flickering light of the oil lamps, a thought struck me with such power, with such conviction, that I had no room in my mind for anything else.

I wanted to rush out of the room, out of the palace, and down to the little house near the bazaar where I knew Nasir lived. I wanted to rush into his room, shake him awake, and confront him with the notion that had just shaken me to the very bottom of my soul.

But I did not. Suppose I was wrong. If I were, what would he make of my accusation? He would be afraid of what I was saying, of what such a statement might imply. I would surely lose his friendship, his love, forever. I could not bear that.

Yet my idea must be true. There could be no other explanation for what had happened between us in the darkness the previous night—no other explanation that I could accept.

And yet again, how could it be? Everything I knew about women, all my experience of them, denied such a possibility. For after all, Nasir was first and foremost my friend. Therefore what I suspected could not be true. For if it were true, he could not be my friend. In spite of what he had said, he could not be my friend.

It seemed I was destined to be wrong no matter in which direction I turned. My heart insisted on a truth my mind denied. To mention it to Nasir was to risk the loss of his friendship, especially if my mind, and not my heart, proved correct. Before I dared to say a word to him about my suspicions, I must prove them either wrong or right, beyond the shadow of a doubt. And I must prove them without Nasir's suspecting that I was putting him to a test.

The next morning I rode out beyond the city. There I met Amin and Uthman, as we had arranged several days before. We carried bows and arrows with us. We were to hunt pigeons. They were not the most exciting prey, but we could go after them without the company of an entire entourage. We hunted them often when we sought a quick morning's exercise.

Amin and Uthman were successful that day. Amin bagged three birds and Uthman two. I, of course, shot none. I could not have hit the side of a house an arrow's length away that morning.

As we always did, when noon came, we rested in the shade of a rock. We built a fire. Uthman plucked a couple of the pigeons, and we roasted them for our lunch. Usually that meal was more delicious to me than all the sauces and sweets of my father's table. That day I barely nibbled a morsel.

"What's the matter with you, my prince?" Amin asked. "No matter how great your melancholy, your appetite has never suffered before. What's got into you today?"

"Something has," Uthman agreed. "You're the best shot of the three of us. Today you couldn't have hit a stable door."

It seemed as good a time to begin as any. "There *is* something on my mind," I admitted. "It's so strange, so bizarre, I hesitate to mention it to you. You'll find the idea laughable."

"Try us," Uthman said. "I for one, my lord, can't imagine laughing at any words of yours."

"Unless you intend them to be funny," Amin amended.

"Well," I said, "you'll decide what you think I mean, since I don't seem to know myself." I turned from one of them to the other. From my tone they had grasped the depth of my concern, so they had pasted serious, attentive expressions on their faces, Uthman's sincere, Amin's faintly ironic.

"Nasir is our good companion," I began.

"By my father's head!" Amin exclaimed. "I thought you had some great revelation to make to us."

"Be quiet," Uthman remonstrated. "Give Mahmud a chance."

I spoke again. "Have you ever noticed anything odd about Nasir?"

"Odd?" Uthman asked. "How do you mean, odd?"

"Different. Different from us."

"He's richer," Amin said drily. "Perhaps even richer than you, my lord. His perfection gets on my nerves. It isn't human."

"Anything else, Amin? Anything else?" I stared at him intently.

"Why do you ask me?" Amin replied testily. "He's more your friend or Uthman's than he is mine."

"Because of things you said to him—things you said to him the night that he and I first walked together, without you and Uthman."

Amin's face grew dark. "That was an evil night," he said. "I spoke out of turn."

"Did you?" I asked. "Perhaps you suspected something Uthman and I chose to ignore."

"You can't be saying what I think you're saying," Amin whispered.

"Yes, I am," I returned.

"Well, then, say it," Uthman cried impatiently. "I don't know what you're talking about."

I picked up a stick and began to draw circles in the sand. "I think," I said very slowly, very clearly, "I think Nasir is not Nasir at all. I think Nasir is a woman!"

Uthman rose from his cross-legged position in front of the fire and knelt beside me. "My lord," he said softly, "the pressures of state business have been very great lately. You've been tired, distracted. When a person feels that way, it's only natural for his mind to be prey now and then to wild imaginings."

I reached out and grasped Uthman's arm. "It's not my imagination, Uthman. It's a feeling. It comes from deep inside me. It's the only explanation I have for what happens to me sometimes when I'm with Nasir. Not all the time, but sometimes."

Amin's voice was carefully expressionless as he spoke. "It would explain a lot," he said. "It would explain his never going to the bath with us. It would explain why he never hunts with us—not for pigeons or gazelles or anything else."

"On the other hand," Uthman insisted, "there's much more about Nasir that makes such an idea absurd. He's a merchant. Actually, he's a great merchant. There are other men in this world whose interest in women is limited. I've heard of such things, and so have you. Most of those men are less honest than Nasir and pretend to a prowess they don't have, that's all. But I've never heard of a woman making a profit of twenty thousand dinars in six months' time. Women don't have the kind of mind that success in business requires. Women are not—" He paused, struggling for the right word. "They're not geniuses. Beautiful, good, loving, perhaps even occasionally clever—but brilliant, never. Not in that way. Not in the way of business."

"Ask him, my lord," Amin said. "That's all. Just ask him."

"Oh, come on, Amin," I protested, "I can't do that. If I'm wrong, he'll never speak to me again."

Amin merely smiled.

"You mean," Uthman said, "you're not sure."

"That's right," I agreed. "I'm not sure. I feel in my heart that it's so, but what you say, Uthman, is also true. No one I know has a mind more masculine than Nasir's."

"All right, then," Amin said brightly, "you have another choice. Test Nasir."

"Yes, Amin, that's what I must do. What do you suggest?"

Amin stroked his goatlike beard. "Challenge Nasir to a game of chess. There isn't a woman in the world who knows how to play chess."

"He's very good at backgammon," I reminded him doubtfully.

"Backgammon is largely luck," Uthman interjected. "Chess is all skill. Women don't play chess. Have you ever heard of it?"

Uthman was right. Women did not play chess. It seemed a clever and easy solution. My mind was at ease for the first time in three days. I attacked what was left of the pigeons with relish. After we had eaten, we mounted our horses and rode back to the city.

That evening we met, as we sometimes did, at a gaming house. Nasir was to join us, but he was late. By the time he arrived, I had already sent the servant for chessboards rather than our usual backgammon boards. Two of them were set out on the low table in front of us. Amin and Uthman had embarked upon a game. When I caught sight of Nasir in the doorway,

I waved at him with an eagerness I suddenly did not feel. A part of me did not want to know the answer to my question. If Nasir proved to be other than what he appeared, I would have lost my friend. If he proved to be just what he seemed to be, I would have lost—what? I was not sure, but I suspected that the love of women would hold no allure for me for a long, long time. There could be no winner at the game I was setting out to play, and I had not realized it until the moment I caught sight of him.

But it was too late to stop what I had begun. Nasir's face lit up when he saw the chessboard, with the black and white ivory chessmen ranged in neat rows on the black and white squares. "I haven't played chess in more than a year," he cried. "You'll win easily, my lord. I've probably forgotten all I ever knew. My mind is desperate for the exercise."

"I didn't know you were so fond of chess," I replied drily. "You should have said something before this."

"Chess isn't as good for gambling as backgammon," he said as he took the seat opposite me.

"But let's put a little wager on the game anyway," I suggested.

"Why not? How much?"

"Five dinars."

Nasir's eyebrows shot up. It was a large sum, far more than we'd ever bet on the throw of the backgammon dice. Then he smiled and shrugged. "Why not?"

he repeated. If he was concerned about his skill at the game, there was no doubt of his skill at dissembling.

We began to play. Amin and Uthman soon gave up the pretense of carrying on with their own game and watched us intently. After the first few moments, it was perfectly clear that Nasir knew what he was doing. Talking ceased. No more suggestions from Uthman, no more jokes from Amin. We were surrounded by silence. We must have played for more than an hour—not an unconscionable length of time for a game of chess, but long enough to prove that we were quite evenly matched. Then, because I could see only ten moves ahead, and Nasir could see twenty, he captured my queen. A few minutes later it was check, and then mate. Nasir had won.

A man. Nasir was a man. That night as we had walked on the quay, I had been dreaming. I had proved that to myself now. I forced a smile to my lips. "Good game, my friend," I said. "We must play again." I reached into my money belt and counted out five gold dinars. Nasir held out his hand. As I placed the money in his palm, our fingers touched. A spark seemed to leap between us. My hand trembled, and so did his.

At that moment I realized I knew no more than I had known before. The next morning, early, after another sleepless night, I sent for Amin and Uthman. They met me in my private apartments. I did not even greet them. "The chess game proved nothing," I said as soon as I laid eyes on them.

"My lord," Uthman cried, "how can you not be satisfied? Surely it's perfectly clear now that Nasir is just who he says he is."

"There's nothing in nature that says a woman can't play chess," I replied. "Nothing, nothing at all."

"All right, all right," Uthman responded with equal fervor. "If a woman can play chess, it's not a miracle. Allah didn't intervene directly to make it happen. But it isn't natural. It's a freak. Nasir is no freak. How can you even think it?"

Amin was pacing up and down, apparently lost in thought, his hand stroking his beard. Miserable as I was, I could not help but smile at the sight of Amin thinking. He looked like a monkey mimicking a man, as monkeys are wont to do. I indulged his little performance for a few minutes and then I called out, "O sage, cease your pacing. The time has come to grant us poor ordinary mortals a taste of the wisdom with which Allah, in his beneficence, has blessed you."

Amin stood still in front of me, and then threw himself to his knees, bending his back until his forehead touched the ground. Now he was playing the part of the devoted courtier. "Amin, get up," I said. "Who do you think you are, a slave? You're a free citizen of Tyre, so stop the games and tell me what you're thinking."

Amin raised himself to a sitting position, crossing his legs tailor fashion. Facing him, I leaned against an array of silk cushions. Uthman was seated on my right side. "Listen, my lord," Amin said in quite his normal tone. "So the chess test wasn't decisive. I've thought of one that is absolutely foolproof. Take Nasir down to the vaults beneath the palace. Show him the armor and the jewels your family's been collecting ever since that merchant-prince, your grandfather, became the greatest man in Tyre."

"But the collections were begun long before that," I mused. "They were begun by his grandfather. We go back a long way on this coast."

"What difference does that make?" Uthman interrupted impatiently. "If Nasir is more interested in jewelry than in armor, you'll know he isn't what he appears to be. If he's more interested in armor than jewelry, you'll know he is who he says he is."

"Yes, that's right," Amin said. "That's the idea."

As before, my feelings about subjecting Nasir to such a test were nothing but confusion. I longed to know the truth, but whatever truth I confronted would be an unhappy truth. I was even more concerned about the way in which I was seeking the truth—by deceit and trickery. Was that a way to treat a friend? But if Nasir was indeed a woman, if he had been deceiving me, and Amin and Uthman—and all of Tyre—for over a year, was he entitled to anything other than trickery and deceit in return? On the other hand, if he was not lying, if he was who he said he was, then what was I doing to the man who was my friend?

However, as before, once the game was launched,

I was unable to pull back. I could not have stopped it if I had wanted to, and I was not sure I wanted to. That evening when the four of us met in Nasir's shop, Uthman mentioned the enormous topaz his father had sold my father the previous week. Amin announced his regret at never having seen it, and I immediately responded with an invitation to all three of them to view the topaz and all the other treasures in my family's vaults beneath the palace. We wasted no time. We arranged to meet the very next day, not in one of the shops, but at the palace.

Late the next afternoon, the three of them gathered in my rooms. Four armed guards accompanied us through the damp, narrow, subterranean passageway that led to the vaults, which were really caves hollowed out of bedrock and fitted with storage chests and cabinets by my wily ancestor. The narrow entrance to the caves was guarded by a small company of soldiers ranged along the passageway, spears and shields always at the ready. Even though he knew perfectly well who I was, the grizzled old captain of the guard inspected the pass impressed with my father's seal for a full five minutes before he let me through. My poor friends had a harder time. Their passes also bore my father's personal seal, for without such a document there was no admission at all to the caves. But that did not stop the old captain from grilling Amin, Uthman, and Nasir for half an hour, as if they were sus-

ected thieves. I let it go on right to the end. It made
a visit to the vaults that much more impressive.

When all four of us were at last through the iron
gate that separated the cave from the passage, I went
immediately to the chest where the topaz was stored,
since seeing it was the ostensible purpose of our visit.
Gold chains, emeralds, and rubies set in rings, silver
collars studded with lapis and massive turquoise, and
pearls as big as marbles filled the chest to the brim.

I held the topaz in my hand so the others could
see it. It was as large as a harem lady's hand mirror and
it sparkled with the reflected light of the oil lamps,
which provided the vault's illumination. Uthman stood
back, having seen it before, many times. Amin and
Nasir leaned in close. "It's magnificent," Amin said.
"I've never seen anything like it."

Nasir murmured a polite assent and then turned
his head to glance at some of the other treasures lining
the walls of the cave.

"Uthman," Amin said, "the topaz is only the
beginning." He picked up an ancient Egyptian diadem
in which the gold had been worked into the shape of
an asp. "Look at this workmanship."

"Nasir, come here," Uthman urged. "It's remarkable. My father would give his fortune to have
something like this to sell."

But Nasir had wandered away from the chest full
of jewels. He was gazing in apparent fascination at a

wall hung with fifteen jewel-studded swords. "By my father's head," he called out in awed tones, "where did these come from?"

With a flick of my wrist, I slammed the chest shut. Quickly I walked across the room and stood at Nasir's side. "Each sword," I explained, "was the most treasured possession of some Bedouin warrior. By rights they should have been buried with their owners when they died, but they were too beautiful for that. Instead, they're kept here, as an inspiration to less warlike types, like me."

"And if there's a war, will you use them?" Nasir asked. His voice sounded eager.

"I don't know," I said. "There hasn't been a war in years. We're peaceful traders here. It suits the whole world to let that be. It suits the whole world that this particular port on the Mediterranean is always open, always available." My voice rose as my annoyance with him increased. "I hope that never changes. So far as I'm concerned, if there's never another war, it won't be too soon!"

I turned my back on Nasir and stalked out of the cave. But he hurried after me. "My lord, my lord," he cried as he caught up to me, "do you think I'm sanguine? Do you think I'm one of those foolish men who's never fought a war and therefore thinks nothing could be more marvelous?"

"I don't know," I replied sharply. "I only know

one day I'll be wali, and I'll think very hard before I spill the blood of the men of Tyre."

"If honor or policy demands it, you'll do it," he replied. "I know that war isn't begun lightly, but no city can avoid a war unless it's prepared to fight one if necessary."

"That's true." I sighed. "Unpleasant, but true."

Amin and Uthman followed us. The gate clanged shut once we were all in the passageway, which was too narrow for two people to walk side by side. I lengthened my stride and moved away from the others as fast as I could. I was taller than the other three and my legs were much longer, so I was soon far ahead of them. When I reached the stairway that led back up into the palace, I turned and called to them, still halfway down the passage. "Good night," I said. "I'll see you tomorrow." I rushed up the stairs and then, moving as quickly as my dignity and my position would allow, I hurried to my own apartments. I did not want to see them. I did not want to talk to them. I was sick at heart.

I knew now that I had wanted Nasir to be a woman. I had wanted him to be a woman so that I could love him as a man loves a woman and at the same time love him as a man loves his friend. And my disappointment in realizing that he was not a woman, that he could not be a woman, was so great that I was filled with a terrible bitterness, an awful sorrow. I wanted to speak to no one. I wanted to look at no one. Though wine is forbidden to the followers of Mohammed, we kept some in the palace with which to entertain our frequent Christian, Jewish, and pagan guests. I sent for a bottle, drained it to the dregs, and then I went to sleep.

When I awoke the next day, the noon sun was streaming through my windows. My head ached, my tongue was thick with fur, my lips were as dry as if I'd been waterless in the desert for a week. I could barely move myself, but Faris, who watched me while I slept, noticed the first flicker of my eyelids. "My lord . . ." he whispered.

"Shush," I cried. "Why are you screaming?"

"I am not, my lord," he replied, stung.

I shut my eyes against the glare of the light. It was not Faris who spoke too loudly, or the sun that shone too brightly. They were the same as they always were; it was my own head that was different. It ached so much from the wine I had drunk that I would have raised no objection if a soldier bearing one of the Bedouin swords had walked in the room at that very moment and chopped it off.

I sat up very slowly and very slowly opened my eyes. My stomach turned over three times and threatened to eject its contents all over my cushions. I swallowed hard, and triumphed over it, momentarily at least. "Who gave you leave to wake me at such an unholy hour?" I scolded.

"It's noon, my lord," Faris replied. "I saw you move and thought you were awake. Your friends await you in your reception room."

"Friends? Which friends?" Had Nasir come to tell me something? But what could he have to tell me? He did not know I had any questions. And anyway, did I want to talk to him? I was in no condition to talk to anyone. But if I put him off, perhaps he would not come again.

"The lord Amin," my servant replied, "and the lord Uthman."

I sighed. "They are neither of them lords." I leaned back among my pillows. "Send them in. But bring me a basin first, so I can wash."

With Faris's aid, I made myself presentable. Then he left the room. A few moments later he ushered Amin and Uthman before me, and then, at my signal, he withdrew.

My friends made themselves comfortable on some cushions. "Your face looks like a baboon's rear end," Amin announced cheerfully. "I never saw anyone look worse. What did you do to yourself after you ran away from us?"

"Drank myself into a stupor," I replied shortly.

"But why?" Uthman replied. "What did we do?"

"It wasn't us, you fool," Amin replied. "It was Nasir. All that warlike talk proved to Mahmud that he is not a woman; and for some reason or other, a woman is what your prince wants Nasir to be. If I'd known the trouble Nasir was going to cause, I'd have pushed him into the sea the first day I set eyes on him." Though Amin smiled as he spoke, something in his tone of voice told me he was not joking.

"I don't want Nasir to be anything but what he is," I said. "I just want to know."

"Well," Uthman responded reasonably, "now you do know."

"But you don't know, do you?" Amin said with an ironic laugh. "You're still not satisfied."

"But why not?" Uthman asked. "Yesterday proved beyond the shadow of a doubt that Nasir is what he says he is."

"Words," Amin murmured. "Just words. Words prove nothing."

"Well, then," Uthman demanded, "what does?"

I had not been paying much attention to their argument, but Amin's next words cut through my foggy brain like a knife through an apple. "We can't deny what we see. Nasir's naked body will be proof enough even for Mahmud." He turned to me and looked directly into my eyes. "Would it not, my prince?" he asked quietly.

I nodded slowly.

"Invite Nasir to the bath, my lord," Amin continued. "Demand that he accompany you, as befits a friend. If he won't, then he's no true friend of yours."

"Amin," I said, "fetch him. Tell him I'm ill and that he must come to see me. But tell him no more than that. Uthman, you can go with Amin, but keep your mouth shut."

Poor Uthman. He looked as if someone had just thrown a pail of cold water in his face for no reason at all. He did not understand what was happening. But Amin did.

While they were gone, I planned the course of the conversation I would have with Nasir. It would be subtle; Nasir would never suspect that I had a hidden motive for my insistence. I was so pleased with my cleverness that my headache and my nausea disappeared entirely. When Nasir came into my room, I actually had to pretend that I was not feeling well.

The three of them entered together. Nasir instantly knelt down beside me. Amin and Uthman withdrew discreetly and seated themselves in the window. Nasir and I spoke in such low tones that they could not hear us.

"My lord, you were in perfect health yesterday," Nasir said, a frown creasing his forehead. "What struck you down so suddenly?"

"Oh, it's nothing, my friend." Though my words were dismissive, I made sure that my voice was faint and trembling. "Just a passing fever. It will go as it came. And if it doesn't—well, that too will be Allah's will."

"My lord," Nasir cried, "don't say such things!" His cool hand grasped mine and held it for a moment.

I withdrew my hand from his as quickly as if I

had just touched fire. After all, I had no fever whatsoever, and I did not want him to have the opportunity to figure that out. "Don't touch me," I whispered. "I don't want you to catch what I've got."

"Of course," Nasir added thoughtfully, "you probably were coming down with it yesterday. You acted very strange. You left us so abruptly."

"Please accept my apology. I'm sure it was the fever working on me, and I didn't even know it."

"Oh, my lord, no apologies are required." His voice was thick with anxiety. "My father had a fever not so long ago. He nearly died."

I was causing Nasir pain and for no reason at all. But that wasn't true, I told myself. There was a reason; there was. "What can I do for you?" he begged. "Where are your attendants? Why aren't you being properly nursed?"

"Everything's being done," I assured him. "I sent them away. I didn't want them here when my friends were here. The room gets so crowded, and I feel as if I'm suffocating." I coughed mightily, and then gasped, as if fluid in my chest were making it difficult for me to breathe.

Immediately Nasir was behind me, plumping my pillows and readjusting them, in an effort to relieve my spasm. "It's all right, my friend," I whispered. "It's passed. In a few days, I'll be like new again. I'll be back in the shop, losing to you in backgammon and chess as usual."

"Ah, my lord," said Nasir with a small smile, "I promise you that when you return, you'll win. You'll win every game."

This was going to be even easier than I had thought. "And we'll take long walks on the quay at night," I said. "We'll walk and walk and talk and talk until the first light of dawn streaks the sky."

"We'll talk about everything," Nasir agreed eagerly. "You'll know everything that's in my heart, and I'll know everything that's in yours."

"We'll go to the bath together," I continued in the same faint, dreaming tone. "We'll lie side by side in the steam room as the masseurs rub the weariness out of our muscles. We've never done that," I reminded him. "You've never had the time. But you'll have the time now, won't you? You won't let business stand in the way of friendship any more."

"I don't want to deny you anything, my lord," Nasir whispered, his voice so soft I could barely hear him.

I smiled. "Good," I said. "I'll remember that." I leaned back against my pillows and shut my eyes. "I'm so tired now, I need to sleep. I thank you for coming, my dear friend, my other self."

"Rest well, my lord." Again, his hand grasped mine. I heard the rustle of his jubba as he rose. I heard his footsteps as he crossed the floor to join Amin and Uthman by the window. Then I heard the footsteps of all three of them as they tiptoed wordlessly out of the room.

For three days I remained in bed. I ordered a guard to stand before my door and say to anyone who inquired after me that I was too ill to receive visitors. Faris and Abdullah no doubt realized that I was healthy as a horse; but if I said I was sick, they dared not say otherwise. They were the only people who saw me. My father was hunting gazelles from his lodge in the Lebanon mountains. He was the only man who would have shouldered his way past my guard without my permission.

On the morning of the fourth day, I rose from the bed as soon as I awakened. I shook Faris, who was dozing beside me. "Wake up, dreamer," I cried. "I'm so hungry, I'll eat you if my breakfast isn't here in three minutes."

"Thanks be to Allah," Faris murmured, casting his eyes downward in mock humility. "My lord has recovered from the mysterious ailment that afflicted him so suddenly."

I grinned and shook him by the shoulder. "Not so mysterious," I admitted. "But I can trust you to say nothing about it."

Faris rose to his feet. "About what, my lord? You were ill, and now you're better."

I nodded. "That's what you'll tell anyone who asks. Now, you'll bring me some bread and fruit. After you've done that, you'll seek out my friend Nasir at the shop he shares with Jihha. You know the shop of Jihha?"

"I know the shop of Jihha," Faris replied. "I've gone there with you often enough."

"Tell Nasir I hold him to his promise to meet me at the bath as soon as I recovered. Tell him I expect him there this afternoon, right after midday prayers." The muezzins called for prayers from the minarets of every mosque in the city. Nasir would not have the excuse of mistaking the time. "Tell him that after being shut inside for three days, I long to mingle with other men, and that I long also for his companionship. Do you have all of that?"

Faris bowed. "Yes, my prince."

"Say this too," I added carefully, "but say it as if it came from yourself. Remind him that his promise was made to me while I lay on the deathbed from which I have miraculously risen, and that if he denies me, he risks the loss of my friendship forever."

Faris bowed again. His face was impassive as usual, but I knew him very well, and I noticed, as he lifted his head from the bow, that he glanced at me quickly and quizzically. Either he did not understand what was going on, or he understood and did not like it. But whatever he thought, he would keep his thoughts to himself and do as he was told. That was Faris's great virtue. I saw to it that he was better paid than any other servant in the palace. His discretion was absolute, as was his devotion.

PART TWO

The morning was endless. I should have received petitioners, as was my duty in my father's absence. My supposed illness had excused me from the tedious task the previous three days, and I had Abdullah inform the vizier that I was still too weak to sit in a hot room for four hours listening to an endless string of petty complaints. "Tomorrow," I said. "Tell the vizier I'll come tomorrow."

But later I was sorry that I had not attended to my work. At least it would have passed the time. I could not concentrate sufficiently to read to myself. I sent for a book, but the tales in it seemed boring and stupid compared to the one that I was living through. I shoved the book aside and considered sending for Amin and Uthman. Amin would have amused me with his jokes, Uthman with his utter seriousness. But they would also have talked about Nasir and the final test. I did not want to talk about it, though it was all I could think about. Finally, I walked in the garden. Fortunately, it is a very large garden. I circled it five times, engaging each gardener I encountered in a lengthy conversation on the care and habits of the plants he tended. They were all pleased. I had never evinced much interest in botany before.

At last it was time to go to the bathhouse—or nearly time. I would be early, I knew, but that was all right. I could sit on a mat in the shade of the palm tree that grew in the courtyard and wait for Nasir there.

But no sooner had I entered the building than the

attendant noticed me. He hurried forward and bowed low. "Mawlana al-amir," he said, "I have a message for you."

"A message?" I felt my bones turn to milk. Nasir had sent an excuse. The excuse meant my suspicions were true. But in a flash I realized that knowing would leave me worse off than before. Could I confront him, calling him a liar? No. I would simply be forced to end our friendship because I had made such an issue of his appearance at the bath. I had said that if he did not come, he was no friend of mine. Had Amin, when he suggested the plan, seen all the way to this inevitable outcome? And how was it that I, Mahmud, son of the Wali of Tyre, had not?

"What's the message?" I asked, keeping my voice calm. But my fists were clenched, my nails digging into my palms.

"Your friend Nasir came by, oh, I guess it was . . . well, midmorning. Yes, I think that's right. Midmorning. He said to tell you this, these very words." The old man paused portentously.

"Yes?" I urged impatiently. "The words, the very words?"

"Let me see." The old man scratched his head. "My memory isn't what it used to be. But still, it isn't bad for a man my age. These were his words, his very words." He said them in a loud, reverberating voice, as if he were reading a proclamation in a public square. " 'I came for a purpose, and I left for a reason.' " The

131

old man smiled and nodded his head quickly several times, obviously pleased with himself.

"That's all?" I asked. "That's all he said?"

"Well, he said more. Of course he said more. He said 'Peace be with you, Grandfather.' And he said, 'Do you know Prince Mahmud?' A foolish question, I told him. Who in Tyre doesn't know Prince Mahmud? And then he said, 'The prince will come here about noon. I want you to give him a message.' He repeated the message half a dozen times, and he made me repeat it too. He gave me a whole dinar." The old man pulled the coin from the pocket of his trousers and rubbed it gleefully. It was probably the most money he had ever held in his hand at one time in his life. " 'I came for a purpose, and I left for a reason,' " he repeated. "That's all. 'I came for a purpose, and I left for a reason.' "

"By my father's head," I cried, "I am a fool. I am the worst fool to ever walk the earth."

I turned as if to leave, but the old man put his hand on my shoulder. I faced him again. "Your friend said to give you this," he said. And into my hand he put a chess piece, a white queen. If I had not been sure before, I was sure now. With a cry like a wounded lion's, I rushed out of the bathhouse as fast as my feet could carry me.

Faris ran after me. He had to run fast to keep up with me, and he was really too old for so much activity.

By the time we reached the quay, he was flushed and breathless, his usual dignity dissolved in perspiration.

But I had no time to worry about Faris. It took me only a few minutes to find the harbor master. He was standing at the end of one of the docks, directing the unloading of a ship carrying linen and rice from Egypt. He saw me running toward him and shook his head, amazed. "Prince Mahmud," he cried when I stood next to him, "what's the matter? You look like a wild man. What's happened, mawlana?"

Several ships lay at anchor in the harbor. With a wave of my hand, I took them all in. "Did you see a woman board any of these ships in the last hour or so?" I asked. "She was probably carrying a good deal of luggage."

The harbor master nodded. "I saw such a woman," he said. "But she's not aboard any of the ships still at anchor." He pointed out to sea. My eyes followed his finger, and far off, beyond the breakwater, against the horizon, I could make out a sail. "She boarded that ship, my lord," the harbor master explained. "About an hour ago she came down and boarded the *al-Fustat*. It was ready to sail, waiting only for her. It set off immediately, and the breeze is so stiff it's made very good progress."

"Who was she?" I begged desperately. "Who was that woman?"

"My lord, it seems you would know that better

than I," he replied calmly. "I don't know who she was. I never saw her before in my life, at least not so far as I know. She was heavily veiled."

I struck the side of my head with my hand three times. "Fool," I sputtered. "Fool. Fool."

The harbor master stiffened. "Who's a fool, my lord?" he asked sharply.

"Me," I assured him. "Only me. Where's that ship going? The one upon which the woman set sail?"

"To Alexandria, my lord," the harbor master replied.

"Then I must go to Alexandria too. Which of these other ships sails for Alexandria?"

The harbor master shook his head. "None, my lord," he said. "We don't expect another ship to sail for Alexandria within the week. The one we're unloading just came back from there, and the *al-Fustat* just set out."

"But I must go to Alexandria," I insisted. "We'll make one of my father's dhows ready to sail. How quickly can that be done?"

"Three days, at the very least, mawlana," the harbor master replied. He stared at me, frank curiosity in his eyes. He must have thought I had lost my mind. Well, in a way I had. "It'll cost money."

"Faris will get you what you need. If you can have the ship ready to sail in less than three days, there'll be ten dinars in it for you." I turned toward Faris. "Stay here and assist him," I ordered.

"But my lord . . ." Faris, the perfect servant, dared to protest. "I don't think I should leave you."

"I'm all right," I assured him. "Truly, I am. And I'll tell you exactly where I'm going. You can come for me there later. I'm going to the gaming house. Amin and Uthman will be there. They'll look after me."

Mollified, he bowed his assent. I left the harbor and pushed my way through the streets with slow, heavy steps. There was, it seemed, a mountain on my back.

Amin and Uthman were waiting for me. They realized instantly the significance of the fact that Nasir was not with me. Amin started talking even before I sat down. "He didn't come. He made some excuse."

I nodded briefly.

"Well, now you know." Amin sighed and smiled at the same time. "Now you're satisfied. Your suspicions were correct. You can forget Nasir. He doesn't exist. We can go back now to the way it was. We can go back to just the three of us."

"What are you talking about, Amin?" I shook my head slowly. I could not believe what my ears were hearing. "You don't understand. I thought you did, even if you didn't like it. But you understand least of all."

Amin stared at me blankly.

"Listen to me, Amin," I said slowly. "Listen to me very carefully. Nothing is the same. Nothing will ever be the same again. There lives on this earth a woman who can be my friend and my lover. Do you understand that? Do you understand what a marvelous thing that is?"

"A friend is a friend," Uthman interrupted, "and a woman is a woman. You can't have them in one person. The whole world knows that."

"If that's what the whole world knows," I announced emphatically, "then the whole world is wrong. I believed the whole world, and I lost her. I didn't trust my own instincts, and now she's gone. She's left Tyre."

"You're well rid of her," Amin insisted. It was as if he had not heard a single word I had said. "She's a freak, but she's a woman too, and like all women, she's a deceiver."

"Who knows what reasons she had for her pretense?" I retorted. "Who knows what poverty or what threat drove her to do what she did? And now, by leaving this white queen behind, she reveals all. But for my deceit, there was no reason—no reason whatsoever." My fingers moved over the carved surface of the chess piece I held in my hand. "I had only to confront her honestly with what my body, my heart, and my soul told me to be true. If I'd trusted myself, she'd be my affianced bride this very moment. Instead, she's off to Alexandria, and I can't follow for three days." In my despair, I covered my face with my hands.

"Follow her?" Uthman sounded like an idiot. "Follow her?"

"You can't leave Tyre," Amin said. "You're the prince. Your father will never permit it."

I lifted my face from my hands and looked directly at Amin. "A merchant prince, my friend," I reminded him. "In our family, the heir always makes a journey so that he can understand the sources of our wealth. I've delayed mine because my father needs my help here at home. But he knows as well as I do that I must go. I delay no longer. I don't care if I have to scour every city from here to the western ocean. I don't care if I come back with a white beard down to my feet. If she lives, I'll find her and make her my princess."

"You're in love, my lord," Amin sneered. "Take a cold bath and it will pass."

I stood up and grabbed Amin. I pulled him up next to me and put my face very close to his. "You know nothing," I told him. "You're an ignoramus. Haven't you the imagination to think what it will be like to love such a woman? At that moment, our two bodies and our two souls will become one. I would travel to the ends of the earth, I would die, my friend, in search of such a consummation." I pushed him down again into his seat and turned away from both of them.

But I was not halfway across the room when Uthman was at my side. "Please, my lord," he said, "let me come with you. You shouldn't make such a journey alone."

I smiled a little. "I won't be alone, my friend. Faris will come with me, and a whole ship full of sailors. You must stay here. Your father needs you. Allah alone knows how long I'll be gone. But I will never forget that you offered." I embraced him quickly. Then I walked back to the table. I held out my hand.

Amin stared at it.

"Take it," I said. "We've been friends for a long time. Eventually, we'll be able to forgive each other."

He stood up, took my hand, and clasped it tight. "Goodbye, Mahmud," he said. "I'm sorry."

"Goodbye, Amin," I replied. "I pray that some day you too will find what I go to seek."

Amin shook his head. What I was looking for he would never seek. But I left with my head high and my heart singing. My confusion and my melancholy were gone. I knew what I wanted, and I knew what I had to do to find it.

Part 3

YEARS HAVE PASSED since Buran inscribed her tale with her own hand. Ink grows dim and paper crumbles. Some of what she wrote is as sharp and clear as the day she put it down. Other pages are lost forever. But for the one who reads with the heart as much as with the eyes, mysteries dissolve. For such a one, imagination supplies what time has destroyed.

WAS HE REALLY ILL, my prince, or was he just pretending? He'd been testing me for several days. I was sure of that. This fever, this weakness that had suddenly overcome him could be part of the test. On the other hand, I couldn't deny that *something* was wrong. His eyes glittered unnaturally, his hands shook. He may not have been ill, but he was certainly under a great strain, and the effect was the same.

I wanted nothing more than to tell him the truth. I wanted nothing more than to wrap my arms about him, press my body close to his, cover his face with kisses, and then say, "My lord, I am a woman."

But if I said that to him, how he would hate me for my lies and my deceit, he, who was the most honorable of men. He already suspected that I was something different from what I claimed to be. Soon he'd have to know the truth. Then our glorious friendship would be over. It wasn't only the fact that I'd deceived him that would end it. That was bad enough, for he was more than a little pompous, very full of his own position, and wouldn't like to think he'd been made a fool of. But it was also the fact that men and women can't be friends in the way we'd been friends— or, at least so we both had always been told.

And since it would all be over soon, I gave him the promise he wanted. I told him that yes, I would join him at the public bath when he was better. Did he imagine he was being clever in feigning illness to extract such a promise from me? I wondered. We had both involved ourselves in so many layers of deception that it was hard enough for me to tell what I myself was feeling, let alone figure out what was in his mind.

But that's not how it had been in the beginning. In the beginning we'd played backgammon and joked in the shops and walked along the quay in an exchange of feelings and ideas that was as free and open as the companionship between two gulls soaring above the harbor.

Amin and Uthman had been with us all the time at first. But after a while, it was always Mahmud and I who walked side by side in front of the other two, or behind them. It was Mahmud and I who sat opposite each other over the backgammon board, laughing and joking over our own game, oblivious to the one going on alongside of us. And then came the long walks at night, alone together on the quay, Uthman and Amin not there at all, but off in some other place.

Of course, the four of us still spent time together. I bought a horse and rode with them at least twice a week. Gindar and Abu Sinan had been back to Tyre three times since my arrival, and it was Gindar who had served as my riding instructor. He had taught me well. But I never hunted. Managing a bow and arrow from the back of a horse was really a skill that had to be practiced from childhood. Allah be praised, I didn't have to make up excuses for not joining them when they hunted or played polo. They knew I came from a poor family and wouldn't have learned rich men's sports.

One early morning we were riding through low brown hills, which began their rise from the plain about five miles inland. The track was steep and rough, but it was a ride we enjoyed, because it used all our skill and because when we got to the top of the hill, we could see on one side a valley rich with lush green farms and on the other side the stretch of sandy soil along which we had come, the city of Tyre, with its white and blue domes scraping the sky, and beyond that, the sunlight dancing on the sea.

We reached our favorite hilltop and dismounted. Amin and Uthman led the horses to a flat, grassy area where we usually tethered them when we came to this spot, so they could graze while we drank in the view, gossiped, and discussed life's deepest meanings, all at the same time.

Uthman rejoined Mahmud and me quickly, telling us that Amin's horse was in a lather, and that Amin was rubbing him down. I hadn't noticed that Amin's mount had suffered from the uphill climb any more than ours, nor had I ever known Amin to take unusual care of his animal, but at the time I really didn't think anything of it. It was only afterwards that I remembered.

Later, we rode back down. Going up a hill is physically exhausting, but going down is far more dangerous. The track, which wound its way steeply around boulders and clumps of thorn trees, was littered with stones, dead branches, and unexpected swellings of earth. We would have been better off on donkeys than on horses, but of course no young man with a reputation for courage and high spirits would have been caught dead on the back of a donkey.

We were clattering downward single file, Mahmud in the lead, I in the rear, when suddenly I felt my horse's rear right leg give away. The animal collapsed and slid forward, and I was thrown in the bracken on the side of the track. Amin had pulled far ahead of me. It flashed through my mind that Amin was lucky. Had he been close to me, my sliding horse would have crashed into his and sent him flying too.

I let out a scream, a high-pitched scream, as I fell to the earth, not because I was hurt, but because I was so surprised. The others heard me and reined in. I sat up slowly, clutching my arms about me, as if somehow to keep myself safe. I realized that my luck had held.

If I had fallen to the left instead of the right, I could have gone over the edge of a deep ravine, landing in its stony bottom, my arms and legs broken at best, at worst my head split open and my brains spilled all over the sharp-pointed rocks.

In a moment Mahmud was at my side. He put his arm around my shoulder. "Nasir, are you all right?" His voice was breathless with fear and concern. "What happened?"

I shook my head. I didn't know what had happened, not really.

Uthman had grabbed my horse's reins and pulled her to her feet. "She's bruised," he called out, "but no bones seem broken."

"What do I care about the horse?" Mahmud muttered. His hands moved with gentle expertise up and down my arms and legs. "Are you in a lot of pain?" he asked softly. "You don't seem to have broken any bones."

I put my hands on his arms and pushed him away a little. I didn't want him touching me any more than he already had. "I'm all right," I said. "I think I can stand up."

"No, not so fast," Mahmud ordered. "Rest a bit. We don't want you going into shock."

I shivered slightly, my arms still crossed over my breast. He stood up, took off his jubba and wrapped it around me. Uthman approached us. "The horse threw a shoe," he said. "That's why he stumbled."

"Threw a shoe?" I was amazed. "He was at the blacksmith's three days ago. Wait 'til I get my hands on that smith."

"Who is he?" Uthman asked.

He was the smith both Uthman and Amin employed, the one they had suggested to me. "Abu Riad," I said.

Uthman shook his head. "I don't understand. His work for me has always been perfect."

Amin had made his way back up the hill very slowly, but now, at last, he stood behind Uthman. "No one's perfect. Abu Riad can make mistakes, just like the rest of us."

"Not in the practice of his craft," Mahmud countered angrily. "There's no excuse for that. Nasir could have been killed."

"But he wasn't, was he?" Amin said. There was a dryness, a coldness, in his voice that sent a shiver through me, in spite of the extra jubba that Mahmud had wrapped around me.

"Give me your hand," I said to Mahmud. "I'll try to stand now." My prince grasped my fingers firmly in his and pulled me to my feet. I was a little unsteady for a moment and had to lean against him. But I wasn't hurt, only bruised and shaken up. In a moment I could stand alone.

"You can't ride your horse," Uthman said, "not without a shoe. One of us will lead him back, and one of us will ride double with you."

"Nasir will ride with me," Mahmud said. Leaning on him, I picked my way gingerly down the path toward his horse. My legs were still unsteady, and I watched each step my feet were taking. That's why I and not one of the others saw it. "Look!" I exclaimed to Mahmud, pointing. "Look over there. It's the shoe." It was lying in the bracken just a foot or so from the track. It must have tumbled down the hill from the point at which it fell off the horse's hoof and stopped when it struck the boulder against which it was now resting.

"See the shoe?" Mahmud called to Uthman, who was behind us. "See it over there, next to the boulder? Pick it up."

"What for?" Amin asked. "It's of no use."

"Horseshoes are expensive," Mahmud said. "It would be a pity to waste good iron that could be melted down and used again."

Uthman picked up the shoe and brought it over to Mahmud and me. I took it from him. "I'll bring it back to Abu Riad," I said, "when I go to see him to complain about the job he did and ask for my money back." I turned the shoe over in my hand and looked at the nails, jagged and twisted from tearing out of the horse's hoof. But one hole in the shoe had no nail in it at all. Had that been where Abu Riad had made his error, for some reason not hammering a nail through that particular hole? The idea seemed so unlikely I couldn't really credit it. It was simply too obvious an error for a man as experienced as Abu Riad to make. There must have been another reason for the loss of the nail.

Riding behind Mahmud back to the city, I held my body stiff, fearful that even beneath my shirt, my vest, and the jubbas that covered all of that, he would feel my breasts pressed into his back. Actually, my breasts were so small and firm that it was extremely unlikely Mahmud would become aware of them as we trotted across the plain. It was I who was aware of them. It was I who was aware of every nerve in my body, aware of them in a strange, pleasurable, frightening way that had nothing to do with the scratches and bruises I'd suffered in my fall.

Just as I was suddenly (or was it sudden? had it not been creeping up on me for weeks now?) sharply aware of strange sensations in my own body, I was also sharply aware of everything around me. It was as if all of my senses had been honed to a fine edge. Clattering across the plain, far from the sight of the sea, I could nevertheless smell the salt in the fresh wind that blew in my face. I could hear Mahmud's deep, regular breathing even above the noise of the horse's hooves striking against the hard earth. I could see snails crawling in the dirt. And when we returned to the city, to Abu Uthman's stable, I realized that Amin's horse was no more tired, no more lathered and foaming than Mahmud's or Uthman's. His horse had just as much stamina as the others, and if that was so coming back, it had been just as true going up.

Mahmud wanted to send his doctor to me. Of course I would permit no such thing. I assured him that I was fine, and when I dismounted and walked quite easily to my mare's side, grasping her rein in my hand, Mahmud seemed convinced. Amin had led her all the way home and was standing next to her now. "It was odd," I said, keeping my voice very low so that the others couldn't hear, "it was odd that a nail was completely missing from my horse's shoe. It looked as if someone had pulled it clean out with a tool."

"A freakish accident," Amin replied calmly. "An evil omen. You'd better be careful, Nasir. Perhaps your luck is turning. It might be a good time for you to leave Tyre and gather your herbs some place else. Accidents, you know, always come in threes."

"Well, Amin," I replied with equal calmness, "as I wait for the other two, I'll be on my guard. I know now where to look."

"This one could have killed you," Amin replied. "You may not be so fortunate next time."

I looked away from Amin for a moment. Mahmud and Uthman were several yards distant, deep in conversation with Abu Uthman's groom. I turned again to Amin. "Why do you hate me?" I asked.

"Hate you? What a ridiculous thing to say." His voice was empty of emotion. "It was I who introduced you to the best society of our city; I who saw to it that everyone accepted a poor peddler's son as an equal. Even the prince. Even the prince." And he shot me a glance so full of malice that I felt as if he had struck me.

Then I understood. Before I came, Amin had been Mahmud's special friend. My coming hadn't made any difference to Uthman. He had always hovered on the outskirts, and things were the same for him as they'd always been. But I had replaced Amin as the companion of Mahmud's heart. He couldn't forgive me for that.

I had no more to say to Amin. No words of mine were going to make him feel any different about me. All I could do to make him forgive me was leave or separate myself entirely from Mahmud. And for Amin I would do neither. He meant nothing to me. Whatever I did, I would do for Mahmud.

About a month later, on a starless night, Mahmud and I took our last walk along the quay. It was the night that I teased him and ran away from him, the night that he chased me down the harborside and held me pinned against the breakwater wall. When we parted, I said good night to him as cheerfully as I always did. But I had to clench my fists to control my shaking fingers.

When I got back to my room, my own safe little room in Jihha's house, I bade the servant leave the candle, and then I dismissed him. I took off all of my clothes, every single piece, and then I stared down at my naked self. I saw the gentle swell of my two breasts, small, but firm and high, with smooth golden flesh giving way to rosy nipples. I saw the slight curve of my belly, which would never, ever be absolutely flat, no matter how thin and hard the rest of me might be. Beneath my narrow waist, my hips curved like two crescent moons and between my legs black hair curled in tiny ringlets.

I was a woman. I had forgotten that for a long time, and now I knew it again. Mahmud had made me remember. I wasn't angry about it any more. Being a woman hadn't prevented me from doing what I wanted to do. And I wanted to be a woman now—a woman who loved Mahmud and whom Mahmud loved.

But I knew absolutely such a thing could never be. However much I might love Mahmud, his love for me was the love of a friend. If he should ever discover the truth, he wouldn't love me, not even as a friend. He'd despise me for having deceived him. Besides, how could he possibly love me as men love women? My body was thin and tough, not full and seductive. I could make jokes and talk about philosophy, but I was a maid, totally ignorant of the arts of love. What could I offer a man who could call for his pleasure any one of the fifty slave girls who graced his father's palace? If he should ever learn the truth and not despise me, he would merely laugh instead.

If I had known in advance that my disguise would

lead to a completely hopeless passion, would I have put it on? That was an unanswerable question. But I wasn't sorry that I had come to love Mahmud. If Gindar and Jihha had taught me what it was to be a man, then Mahmud had taught me what it was to be a woman. My love for him had taught me finally to know myself.

Poor Amin. If he had only realized it, he had nothing to fear from me. He didn't have to take nails from my horse's shoe or try to drive me away with talk of ill luck and evil omens. Soon enough, I would have to put that distance between me and Mahmud that Amin longed for. I couldn't bear his arm around my shoulder, his hand grasping mine, his face leaning close over the backgammon board, for much longer. The tension would make me explode, and I'd better be gone before that happened.

But I didn't have the courage to leave the very next day. Though I knew that I would have to go soon enough, I hadn't yet become used to the idea of never seeing Mahmud again, of saying goodbye to him forever. A kind of lassitude seized me. I let things drift. I let them take their own course, for just a while longer. For if I couldn't bear to be with him or bear to have him touch me, I couldn't bear to leave him either.

And he didn't know. He didn't know any of this. For the first time in the course of our friendship, I had to disguise my true feelings. I had to keep a secret from him. Of course, I had always kept a secret from him— the secret of my true sex. But oddly enough, I had never thought about that, at least not in the beginning, and not for a long time after the beginning.

I didn't drift for long. The end came quickly, as perhaps, down deep, I'd known it would have to. Mahmud suspected. Perhaps Amin had encouraged his suspicions. I didn't know, and I didn't care. I only knew I couldn't tell him the truth. If I did, he must either despise me or ridicule me, or maybe both at once.

I didn't know the first test was a test until I thought about it later. Mahmud challenged me to a game of chess. My mother had always said that chess was not a game to teach a woman, but how foolish of Mahmud, or Amin, or Uthman, or any man, to assume that just because women as a rule don't play chess, they can't play chess. I won easily. After all, I'd been playing the game against a worthy opponent almost daily since I'd reached the age of ten.

The second test I recognized, and then, looking back, knew the chess game had been a test too. They took me to the vaults and urged me to admire the jewels. I exclaimed instead over the arms. Perhaps I went too far in my enthusiasm. Left to myself, I would have examined the jewels with a professional eye—after all, I dealt sometimes in gems, among many other things—and ignored the armor. In my heart, I cared for neither.

But the third test I couldn't beat. From the third test I could only run away. The moment I had known would come since the last night on the quay was upon me.

After I left Mahmud lying on his supposed sick bed, I went to the shop of a tailor. This shopping trip was precisely the opposite of the one I had made in Baghdad a seeming lifetime before. This time I bought women's clothes instead of men's clothes. This time I spent without thinking, instead of haggling over every copper. Since I wanted the clothes to be ready the very next day, I had to pay a great deal for them, but it didn't matter. I had to be prepared. I imagined Mahmud might recover from his illness with amazing speed.

I went home and sat in my little room, composing a lengthy letter to Jihha, telling him a good deal, but not everything. I counted all the money I kept in a strongbox hidden behind a brick in my bedroom wall. I had long ago paid back to Jihha my share of the initial capital for our venture, and since then we had been dividing all the profits evenly. Jihha had wanted to hold my share, "to keep it safe for you," he had said, but I was too wary to permit that. I trusted him, but only when he wasn't tempted. I put the box back in the wall. Then I went to the shop as usual.

In the next couple of days I made sure all my accounts with Jihha were brought up to date. By offering generous salaries and paying something in advance to their parents, I was able to persuade two of our young porters, Salih and Muhsin, to accompany "my sister" on a long journey as her servants and protectors. I told them to get ready, for the departure would come suddenly and soon.

When Faris came to me with word that Mahmud was better and longed to see me at the bath as I had promised, I was prepared. I went to the bathhouse well before the appointed time and left a talisman for my prince with the attendant. It was my white queen, the one my father had given me when I left Baghdad. It had brought me luck. I prayed it would do the same for Mahmud. I left a message too. "I came for a purpose," I said, "and I left for a reason." He would understand. And if he didn't, it didn't matter. He wouldn't be able to find me, if by some strange chance he should want to. Not even Jihha knew my real name or the name of my native city. Gindar did, because it was Gindar who three times had carried money from me to my father. But Gindar wouldn't be back in Tyre for months. By then Mahmud would have put me out of his mind.

I returned to the house I shared with Jihha. I gave the letter I'd written two days before to the serving boy and told him to give it to Jihha. Then I dressed in the woman's clothes I had picked up at the tailor's the day before. I had told him that they were a gift for my beloved and he had better take great pains to make them magnificent. As I put them on, their filmy silk felt strange against my skin, but not uncomfortable. I veiled my face heavily because I didn't want to be recognized when I went out into the street, and I didn't want to appear anything but a modest woman.

My boys were waiting for me. I had sent for them earlier, and I had packed my things earlier, too. The packing hadn't taken long. I took no clothes, since I had no woman's clothes except the ones on my back. All else I owned was suitable only for a man, and I couldn't be a man any longer. I was done with deception and the trouble it had caused. Not that I regretted my disguise. Without it, I wouldn't have had the courage to do what I had done. But I didn't need it any longer. I had outgrown it. I was Buran now, a woman, and content, in spite of my sorrow, to be so.

The boys picked up my luggage. It consisted of money, essences, medicines, and jewels, though I certainly didn't tell them what my locked cases contained. We went down to the quay and boarded the dhow for Alexandria. It was the only ship leaving port that day. I had booked passage on it earlier that morning, again for "my sister." It seemed important that I leave Tyre immediately, not waiting for Gindar or some other caravan master to depart for Baghdad. I would make my way back home from Alexandria.

We arrived at the dock just in time. The captain had already delayed his departure half an hour and would have waited no longer for us for fear of losing the tide. We set sail immediately.

All day I had accomplished first one task and then the next one and then the next one, without thinking, just making myself move forward on a prescribed path that had to be followed. The activity had been all-consuming. It had wiped out feeling. But now I was still. I stood on the deck, wrapped in a long aba, a cloak, my hands holding onto the railing, my veil blowing in the breeze. I watched the expanse of sea between the boat and the shore grow wider and wider, the ships in the dock grow smaller and smaller, the minarets and domes of the city disappear from my view. With a sudden flash of pain, as if I had put my hand in a fire, I realized that Tyre was lost to me forever. Mahmud was lost to me forever. It was then that I began to cry.

I cried steadily for three days. After Tyre had completely sunk beneath the horizon, gone from sight as thoroughly as if it had never existed, I went down to the little ship's only cabin and stayed there. My servants slept on the deck with the sailors. One of them brought me food three times each day, and then took the tray away, untouched.

But on the fourth morning, as I drifted across the border from sleep into wakefulness, I saw not my shop, nor the quay, nor my little white room, nor the palace of Tyre, nor the deep-set eyes of Mahmud. I saw instead my father's courtyard, and my father's face, smiling as if in welcome, and my sisters sitting in the courtyard too, arrayed in silks and jewels, and daintily picking sweets off a copper tray carried by a servant. I had sent a great deal of money home, secretly and anonymously, though of course my father would have guessed its source. That money would have made the home to which I was returning far different from the one I had left. Perhaps some of my sisters were already married. I couldn't wait to learn all that had happened to them.

Suddenly I was happy, happy to be going home. I had left part of my heart behind me in Tyre, but the other part had never left Baghdad, and that was the part I was going back to retrieve.

I wrapped myself carefully in my aba and my veil, and then I climbed up on the deck. I walked briskly all around it half a dozen times, taking great swallows of the sharp salt air. After that, I went below and ate my breakfast.

"You're better, lady," Salih said when he returned to the cabin and saw the empty tray.

"Yes, Salih, thank you," I replied, smiling.

"I thought at first you were seasick. But Muhsin said no. He said if you were seasick, you would have been throwing up. He said it was something else." Salih was very young. He didn't know yet about the cool remoteness that supposedly characterized a proper servant, like Mahmud's Faris, and I was certainly not the one to teach him. I had hired him because he was very large, very strong, and very willing to knock off the head of anyone foolish enough to look sideways either at me or my boxes.

"Yes, Salih," I said. "It was something else. I'm over it now."

But I wasn't. I'd never be over Mahmud or my love for him. I couldn't imagine marrying another man. Praise Allah, I didn't have to. I could take care of myself. I had been spared a fate I'd always dreaded. I would never have to share the bed of a man I didn't want or who didn't want me.

Our winds were fair, and the journey to Alexandria took us less than a week. When we docked, I remained aboard the ship and sent Muhsin, who was a bit older and a lot sharper than Salih, ashore for information. He returned in a few hours time. "This is a good town," he told me. "The harbor is older and busier than the one at home. Scores of ships and caravans come and go each month, because from here goods are shipped all the way to the west, to Greece and Italy." How mysterious those names sounded to my ears, how romantic and strange. I wondered if there was a market in those places for essences and medicinal herbs. I had caskets of them with me. I knew that once I was back in Baghdad, I'd find a way to continue with my business. My father would help. We'd open up new markets and develop new sources of supply. Some day, years from now, long after Mahmud would be sure to have forgotten his friend Nasir, I could even work again with Jihha. Gindar could be our intermediary.

"In this city of many ships," I said, "I hope there's one leaving soon for Ladhiqiyah or Antioch. I can get a caravan from one of the ports to Baghdad."

Muhsin nodded. "Yes, lady. I found that out in the bazaar. In four days time. I also found a respectable khan and hired a suite of rooms for us."

Muhsin had done a good morning's work. A pang

of regret shot through me, though, as I pictured him wandering freely about the city, questioning stall keepers in the suq, chatting with backgammon players in front of shops, sniffing the morning air without a veil between his nose and its freshness. All that was over for me.

Well, regrets were useless. I had no time for them anyway. I would be busy every moment of my four days in Alexandria. I needed to learn everything about the city and the trading that was carried on from its khans, docks, and warehouses. After all, it was unlikely I would ever be back this way. I had to learn what I needed to know now so that when I was ready to start buying and selling again the information that would put me one step in front of Baghdad's other merchants would already be in my head. Besides, if I kept busy, my mind wouldn't have time for mourning Mahmud. What my heart did was its own concern. Maybe a woman couldn't do business in the courtyard of the khan, but if she were rich enough and shrewd enough, she could hire others to move about for her and get on with her work perfectly well.

Once we were settled in our khan, I sent Salih and Muhsin to a cookshop to order a meal sent around to our rooms. After a week at sea, I longed for ripe, sweet peaches, tender green lettuce, and fresh, untainted lamb's meat. After they'd found some food, I told them they were to search out a tailor. I had nothing more than the clothes on my back, and I knew a woman of my station required an extensive wardrobe. They left, and then I sat, veiled, on the latticed balcony outside our rooms, watching the traffic on the street below. We weren't far from the harbor. I could see ships' masts, sails furled, like tall, thin fingers reaching for the sky. There is something similar—the air, perhaps, or the light—about all towns near the sea. Alexandria was not altogether different from Tyre.

After a while I heard a knock at the door of the room. Salih and Muhsin were still not back. I went to answer it myself, and when I opened it, I saw a young man standing before me. On his head he carried a brass tray laden with covered dishes. He was tall and straight, with finely cut, even features, and a headful of dark curls. He didn't look like a cookshop waiter, though clearly that's what he was.

Suddenly my hand went to my mouth. I had to put it there to keep from crying out. The cookshop waiter, I realized—with a shock that went through my whole body like a bolt of lightning—was my cousin. He was Hassan, eldest of my father's brother's seven sons!

Hassan, a cookshop waiter? Hassan, the marvelous merchant who sent packets of gold home to his father every other week? It was hard for me to believe my eyes, but I knew I must. I would have known Hassan if twenty years instead of three had passed since last I'd seen him. After all, I had thought once that I loved him. That was before I'd learned that love was something more than attraction to a handsome face and an open manner. That was before I'd learned that love was the mingling of two souls.

Two years before, I would have screamed "Hassan!" as soon as I laid eyes on him. But I was wiser now, and skilled at dissembling. I knew he wouldn't recognize me. He hadn't seen me face to face since I was a scrawny eleven-year-old, chasing after him in the courtyard. Now I was a tall, slender, richly dressed woman, my face scarcely discernible beneath layers of golden gauze.

"Set the food on that table," I said, keeping my voice cool and impersonal. "Leave the covers on. I'll wait for my servants to return before I eat."

"Yes, lady," he replied. His voice was polite, but not humble. It wasn't the voice of a man who had been born a servant.

I decided to mention that fact. I crossed the room and stood beside him as he placed the dishes from the tray on the table. "Who are you, young man? You don't have the accent or the carriage of a cookshop waiter."

He straightened himself up and faced me, a glint in his eye, a slight curl to his lips. I realized then that I wasn't the only woman who had noticed his fine dark eyes, his broad muscled shoulders, his long, shapely brown hands. If I had wanted my cousin Hassan, I could have had him at that very moment. He was used to such encounters. But I didn't want him.

"Oh, lady, as you no doubt suspect, I've come

down in the world." His voice was light, as if what he said didn't matter. "I was born a rich man's son."

"And your father lost his money?" That was hard to imagine. My uncle was rich enough to weather years of reverses.

"Oh, no," he replied, still smiling in a way that implied our conversation was about something of no importance. His eyes conveyed the opposite message. "My father's still a rich man."

"And he allows his son to work in a cookhouse?"

"He doesn't know, lady. He lives in another city. I have my pride, lady. I can't ask him for help, and I can't go home again either."

"Why not?" I asked. But I knew my uncle well enough to know why. It wasn't pride that kept Hassan in Alexandria; it was fear.

A frown darkened his face. "Why do you want to know?"

"A story will pass the time." I withdrew a handful of copper coins from my pocket and held them out to him.

He took them. He took them eagerly. I wanted to cry, but I didn't. Instead I sat down and gestured to him to do the same. He told me his story. It wasn't an unusual one. Between gambling and pursuing entertainers, he'd paid little attention to business. His luck changed. He began to lose heavily. Embarrassed to admit the truth, he had spent the money he was supposed to be sending home or using for merchandise to pay his gambling debts or amuse his friends. He neglected the shop, and the people he'd hired to work for him stole from him at every opportunity, and their opportunities were virtually limitless. He guessed what was happening, but didn't have either the desire or the energy to tend to business himself. Soon it was all gone—shop, merchandise, fine clothes, jewels, servants, women, friends, and all. But he knew his father and dared not go home.

When he was done with his tale, his expression lightened. He actually smiled again. "Well, lady," he said, "what do you think of all that?"

"Not much," I replied drily.

"I don't regret it," he assured me. "I had a good time. In some houses in Alexandria, the ladies haven't stopped speaking of me yet. Would you like to know why? For another few coppers. . . ." His voice trailed off suggestively.

My gorge rose into my mouth. So this was what he had come to. For a few more coppers he would sell even himself. Hassan, Hassan, once I thought I loved you. And now? Now I thought of his father and longed to weep.

But none of my feelings were evident in my voice. "Young man," I said, "I'll give you more than a few coppers. I'll give you enough money to buy some merchandise and get yourself honorably home again. What do you think of that?"

A look of perfect amazement passed over his face.

"Allah be praised," he whispered. "I was drowning and now I've been saved." He stood up and walked toward me. "Ah, lady, lady," he whispered, "I will love you as you have never been loved before."

I stood up too, as quickly as I could, and held my hands, palms outward, in front of my body. "You misunderstand me, young man," I said coldly. "I want nothing from you, nothing at all."

"That can't be," he replied. His voice was as dry now as mine. "No one gives anyone anything for nothing."

"Perhaps you're right." A demon had seized me, a mischievous demon. I was possessed of a desire, not for Hassan himself, but for a kind of revenge. He'd laughed at me, and his father had laughed at my father. He'd thought he was better than any of us. I wanted to do something to him that would serve to remind him every day of the week that in truth he was superior to no one. "I'll give you a hundred dinars. What I ask in exchange is so little—really, a price so small as hardly to be considered a price at all."

He shot me a suspicious glance. "And what is that price so small that it's hardly a price at all?"

"My name is Buran," I said. That wouldn't mean anything to him. My name was as common as sand. "I want you to have my initial, 'B,' tattooed just above your heart. That way I know that you'll never forget me. Every time you dress or undress, you'll see my initial and be grateful," I added sweetly.

"Grateful?" he cried. "Grateful? For being branded like a slave? For wearing a mark of shame as long as I live? You can take your hundred dinars and throw it into the sea so far as I'm concerned." But he made no move to leave the room. He just stood there, staring at me, his legs apart, his arms crossed on his chest.

"No one will see the mark," I said. "So what difference can it make in your life? I think you're crazy to throw away a hundred dinars. You must think you're crazy too, a sensible man like yourself. Here's your chance to show everyone what a clever, reasonable fellow you really are."

He dropped his arms to his sides and took a few steps toward me. "Lady," he said, his voice low, "is there no other payment that will satisfy you? Isn't there anything else I can do?"

I shook my head. "Nothing," I said. "I need nothing whatsoever—or at least nothing that you can give me. But I'd like you not to forget me. That would please me. And that's why I ask this very tiny little favor in return for . . . for two hundred dinars."

"You said a hundred just now."

"Did I? I meant two hundred."

He clenched his fists tightly together, unclenched them, and clenched them again. "You see before you a desperate man," he said at last. "I accept your offer."

"That makes me very happy," I said pleasantly. "The giving of charity is commanded by the prophet.

So is gratitude. We are both insuring our entrance into Paradise."

"Lady," Hassan replied quietly, "I don't know what your motive is, but I know perfectly well what it isn't. It isn't to fulfill the commands of Mohammed. Perhaps some man wronged you once, and you take revenge on me instead."

"Well, brother," I pointed out in what I'm sure was a perfectly rational style, "no one is forcing you to accept my offer. If it's revenge I'm after, it's a revenge that costs you almost nothing. On the contrary, you gain enormously."

He didn't reply. There was nothing he could say.

"Return to your cookshop now," I instructed. "Come back in an hour. My servants will be here by then, and they'll see to the details of our transaction."

Which they did, with dispatch, asking no questions and making no comments.

But by the time the four days until the departure of the dhow for Ladhiqiyah had passed, I had changed my mind about returning home immediately. Even for me, two hundred dinars was a lot of money, and I wanted to recoup it. Judicious disposal of some of my jewels had retrieved the two hundred dinars and more. I purchased a cargo of the best sesame oil. It had come from Aleppo by way of Antioch. Baghdad had plenty of its own sesame oil, but I could sell it at a good price in some other city.

It didn't really matter when I arrived home. I had

told my mother I would come when the autumn winds blew a third time. It was not yet summer. Besides, she hadn't really believed me when I had assured her that I would return. No one expected me at any particular moment. No one really expected me at all. And though I longed to see my mother, my father, and my sisters with all my heart, I could postpone that pleasure for a few short months, while I shored up my fortune and experienced who knows what half-expected encounters in other towns.

I didn't see Hassan again after that first day in Alexandria. He probably left for the east on the ship I'd decided not to board. I stayed in the city for about a week, all told, and then I boarded a dhow sailing to Cyprus.

Although I had bought some clothes in Alexandria, my wardrobe was far from complete. One of the first things I did upon arriving in Salamis was visit the shop which, according to the information gleaned by Muhsin in the bazaar, was owned by the best weaver of the many fine weavers in the town and on the small neighboring islands.

The man was in business in a big way. He scarcely put shuttle to loom himself, but instead marched up and down his big storeroom, inspecting the cloth brought to him by women who wove at home, making sure they didn't vary the traditional patterns by so much as a thread. He had assistants too, who waited on the customers thronging his outer rooms, selecting yards of linen from his laden shelves.

Accompanied by Salih and Muhsin, and dressed in trousers and shirt of fine scarlet silk, I entered the shop. One of the assistants caught sight of me as soon as we came through the door. Unceremoniously, he left the man on whom he was waiting and came toward us. With elaborate politeness, he bowed low. "Can I help you, lady?" he asked. "You've come to the right place if you seek the finest woven goods that Cyprus has to offer."

"So I've been told," I replied. "Show me all your patterns."

"Please to make yourself comfortable, lady," he said, escorting me to a kind of alcove equipped with rugs and cushions, where important customers could lounge, sipping cool drinks while the fabrics were brought to them.

The young man scurried back and forth, lugging one bolt after another to show me. So anxious was he to please, so quickly did he move, that sweat soon formed on his upper lip. But I took my time making my choices. I wanted leisure to examine the young man carefully. When he first spoke to me, I suspected who he was. After an hour in his company, I was sure. Though he was only a weaver's assistant, his voice had a nasal superciliousness that condescended even as he was trying to be polite. He walked with a flatfooted gait and his beard grew in sparse pale hairs from his pointed chin. Of all my uncle's sons, he was the one who looked most like his father. He was Hassan's next younger brother, my cousin Ali. I had never liked him.

At last I selected several of the most expensive pieces of material for sale in the shop. And then I said, "Young man, I'll buy all of this stuff on one condition and one condition only. You must deliver it to the khan where I'm staying yourself, after you're done here." I pressed some money into his hand to make sure he agreed. "It'll be worth your while," I added encouragingly.

He didn't fail me. Several hours later, he came just as instructed. Salih and Muhsin were in the other room. As I had with his brother in Alexandria, I told him how surprised I was to discover a man of his obvious rank and ability working as a shopkeeper's assistant. He too admitted that he had come down in the world. It wasn't gambling and women that had been his ruination. He had risked everything he had in backing the expedition of some clever scoundrel who claimed to know the precise location of King Sulayman's mines, which he proposed to reopen. He had showed Ali maps of the route he would follow and supposed samples of the gold and silver lying on the ground in that secret place, just for the taking. Naturally, once he had Ali's money, and the money of who knows how many other poor fools, he had disappeared off the face of the earth.

I made the same offer to Ali that I had made to

Hassan. But I didn't have to increase Ali's bribe from one hundred to two hundred dinars. And Ali didn't blink once at my condition. "Bear your mark to show my gratitude!" he exclaimed. "Lady, I do not need a mark to remember what you are doing for me. I will never forget, but you cannot be sure of that. The condition is, as you say, nothing. No, no, that is not true," he went on, his hands trembling with eagerness. "It is not nothing. It is only right, only correct. I will go out and have it done immediately. I will return for the money before dark." I had never before seen anyone whose eyes glittered so brightly or whose nostrils flared so wide at the thought of a mere hundred dinars. He had the money in cash in his hot hands before dark and so far as I know was gone from Cyprus by dawn.

I remained in Cyprus, buying and selling for another week, and then moved on. I sailed to Sidon on the Lebanese coast, and after several days traveled by caravan inland, back to Damascus, crossing the vast, miraculous garden that careful irrigation had won out of the measureless sweep of desert Arabia, upon whose edge the city perches. The suqs of Damascus were full of ivory-inlaid wood, embroidered damask, Chinese silk, gum Arabic from the south, Indian spices, lapis lazuli and turquoise from central Asia, and pearls from Bahrain. But I concentrated on perfumes and herbs, which were sold there in greater abundance than anywhere else. The herbs sold there now were the same as the ones that were being sold when I visited two years before, but I was different. Now I had things to offer that the Damascan dealers had never heard of. I remained in that marvelous town nearly a month.

What I bought in Damascus I sold first in Tripoli and then in Antioch. Antioch is famous for its vineyards, but there was no demand for wine where I was going, so I left that product for purchase by the traders heading for Egypt and the mysterious foreign cities of the west. Instead, I departed with vials of essence pressed from the lilies that fill the fields surrounding the city, and bales of licorice root.

Finding a caravan traveling from Antioch to Aleppo was easy. I remained in Aleppo several weeks. Using Muhsin and Salih as my go-betweens, I traded briskly with merchants heading south, west, and east. In the course of my six-months' journeying from city to city, I made nearly as much money as I had in the almost two years I'd spent in Tyre.

I had gone to Alexandria by accident. It was the destination of the ship leaving Tyre at the hour I had to depart. I went to Cyprus ostensibly to market a cargo of sesame seed oil, although I had another purpose, which I didn't admit even to myself. But then I went to all those other cities quite consciously aware that I selected them not simply because they were good business towns. I went to them because I knew they were the cities to which my uncle had sent my cousins. And after the accidental encounter with Hassan and the half-accidental encounter with Ali, all the others were as I intended. I looked first in the bazaars, seeking the shops that my cousins were supposed to be running. But I never found them. Then I sent Salih and Muhsin to make inquiries after a young merchant who had arrived a year or two or three before from Baghdad, set up in business, and failed. These inquiries were always successful.

Then I arranged to meet my cousin, always simply as a customer of his employer, always heavily veiled. Each one I rescued as I had rescued Hassan and Ali. Each one carried away from the encounter one hundred or one hundred and fifty or two hundred dinars. And each one carried away as well my initial, the letter "B," tatooed above his heart.

In this way nearly half a year passed. Winter was coming. I had enough money now to support in style for their entire lives my father, my mother, my six sisters, and all the children they would ever bear, to say nothing of myself, who would never bear a child at all. It was time for me to go home.

Baghdad is far from the sea. To reach it, one must cross the desert by caravan. Women, as a rule, don't travel by caravan. Actually, as a rule, they don't travel at all, unless they're princesses sent to marry distant rulers as part of some political alliance. For this reason, when I sought caravan space, there was a high price asked of me. Yet, for a generous consideration, the chief of the caravan traveling from Aleppo to Baghdad allowed me to join him, though I and my servants would remain apart from the others. Eventually, in the darkness, sitting by my campfire, or in the courtyard of a khan, I did carry on conversations with some of my fellow voyagers, calling back and forth to them through the night. They were merchants, like me, and we had a great deal in common. I enjoyed these conversations, and so did they.

One night toward the end of the journey we slept out. A merchant with whom I'd been chatting awkwardly across thirty paces of empty space actually rose from his seat by his fire and walked over to mine. I had removed the veils with which I covered myself during the day, but the light was much too flickering and dim for him to have seen much of me by it. Salih and Muhsin were about their business of tending to the cooking and the animals, but their presence could be felt. "Lady," the merchant asked me, "what's your name, and where are you from?"

"I'm Buran of Baghdad," I replied, "daughter of that Malik known as Abu al-Banat."

"And your husband? Who's he?"

"I have no husband."

"You're a widow then."

"No," I informed him coolly, "a maid."

He wasted no time on preliminaries. "Lady, where in Baghdad can I find your father?"

A curious question. "Why do you want to see my father?"

His tone implied his answer was self-evident. "I

want to ask him to give you in marriage to my son. We'll expect no wedding gifts. Your person will be sufficient."

I laughed out loud. "I'm flattered, brother. My father will be flattered, too. But you know nothing about me. Why do you want me to be your son's wife?"

He sat himself down tailor fashion, with his legs crossed. My fire glowed between us. "I've met women keeping stalls in bazaars," he said. "I've met women from the country selling fruit and vegetables from house to house. But, lady, I have never before met a woman like you. From what you've said, it's clear that you're very rich and that you've earned your money yourself in trade. But not in the buying and selling of peddler's trinkets. You're in business in a big way. My son is useless in business. He needs a wife like you."

"Maybe I'm ugly," I suggested lightly.

"I don't care."

"But, brother, your son certainly will."

My interlocuter began to grow impatient. "He'll do as he's told. Come, Buran, daughter of Malik, tell me where I can find your father once I get to Baghdad."

"He's easy to find. All Baghdad knows the father of seven daughters." Now I let my annoyance show too. "But you can save yourself the trouble. I might be just the wife for your son, but your son certainly doesn't sound as if he's just the husband for me. Actually, I'll probably never marry."

"What?" He sounded as if I'd just surprised him with a blow to the stomach. "That's impossible. That's crazy. Every woman marries, if she can. I'm sure your father will allow you no choice in the matter."

I didn't answer that. I certainly wasn't going to tell a stranger that I could do as I pleased. I couldn't demean my father by saying such a thing. And so I merely replied quietly, "I'm promised. But there are obstacles to the match. Still, I can't marry anyone else until all that is settled." And it'll never be settled, I added to myself.

"I'll seek out your father anyway, once I get to Baghdad," the merchant said, complacency returning to his voice. "After all, no matter how rich and brilliant you are, you can't defy the laws of Allah. Women were meant to marry whomever their fathers decree."

I didn't know where in the Koran those words were written, but I didn't say that out loud either. I rose from my seat by the fire. "We're on our way at daybreak," I said, "so I think, if you don't mind, I'll say good night to you now." I turned away from him and walked toward my animals, hoping by my rudeness to convince him I was no daughter-in-law for him and no wife for his son. I'd never met, never even heard of the boy before that night, but I was already sure he was a worm. The merchant, however, had given me much to think about. I hadn't realized until he approached me that I had become a prize in the matrimonial market.

Another day passed, and then, on the next day,

late in the afternoon, we approached the baked brick walls of Baghdad. Turned a rosy gold by the slanting rays of a dying sun, they looked to me like the jewel-encrusted walls of Paradise. When the caravan reached the bridge, I brought my camel to his knees and dismounted as quickly as shaking hands and beating heart would allow. "Muhsin," I called, "you tend to the luggage and follow when you can." Earlier I had given him careful instructions for finding my father's house. "Salih, come with me." I rushed off with such speed that Salih had to stretch his long legs to catch up with me.

We crossed the bridge. I led the way through the Suq al-Thalatha, and then through crooked, teeming streets into my own neighborhood, Salih close behind me. Disguised as a boy two and a half years before, I had passed through the streets unnoticed in the early morning. Now they were crowded with men on their way home from work and with women bearing bundles and baskets from the bazaar on their heads. This time, although I was respectably veiled, the richness of my clothes attracted more notice than I needed. But I ignored the glances shot at me by passers-by, whether hostile or merely curious. In a few moments I stood before the wall that surrounded our house.

I knew it was our wall because Abu Rashid's and Abu Tahir's houses on either side were exactly as they had been when I left, at least so far as I could tell from the street. But even from the street it was clear that more than a little had happened to the house of Abu al-Banat. The wall had been whitewashed. Large earthenware pots of sweet basil stood at intervals atop it. The squeaking, warped wooden gate had been removed and replaced with a new one of shiny black wrought iron. And wonder of wonders, standing before the gate was a porter! He was a tall, thin man with a scraggly gray beard and pockmarks all over his face, but he held himself erect and wore a disdainful expression that stated clearly that he considered himself to be in the employ of people of importance.

I approached him, Salih close behind me. "Peace be with you," I said quietly. "Permit me, O guardian of the gate, to pass through."

"Who are you?" he asked.

It came as something of a shock to realize that I'd have to identify myself to enter my own father's house. "I'm Buran," I replied. "I've come home."

He shook his head. "No one named Buran lives here," he said.

I felt my heart sink. Had they gone somewhere else to live? I was suddenly tired to death of journeys. I hoped I wouldn't have much difficulty finding them. "Isn't this the dwelling place of Abu al-Banat?" I asked.

He didn't deign to reply out loud, only nodding slightly.

I was relieved. "I think, then," I said firmly, "that you'd better let me pass."

His eyes examined me quickly and thoroughly. They subjected Salih to the same scrutiny. "Well," he said, "I must announce you first." We had passed whatever secret test he was applying to us.

Salih was about to object, but I held up my hand. "It's all right," I told him. "The man is only doing what he's paid to do." But it felt odd to cool my heels on the street in front of my own house.

However, I didn't have long to wait. In a moment the gate flew open, and there stood my father and my mother, smiling and weeping all at once, and crowding them from behind, my sisters.

I forgot my fine clothes and my dignity. I ran toward my father as if I were still the little girl he'd so patiently sat with and taught to play chess. I threw my arms around him, and he held me tight in his. "O daughter, daughter." He sighed, tears running down his cheeks. "I never thought to see you again. Praise Allah, you have come back to us."

We moved into the courtyard. The porter clanged the gate shut behind us. I hugged and kissed my mother and let her stroke my hair and cheeks as she murmured over and over, "I scarcely recognize you. You've grown as beautiful as Fatimah."

Fatimah wasn't there, and neither were Khalidah or Zaynab. I hugged and kissed Sharifah and Aminah and little Darirah, little no longer, but slender and long-legged, with thick black hair that fell to her waist. The first recognizable words I was able to say were,

"Where's Fatimah? Where're Zaynab and Khalidah?"

"O my daughter, sit down and refresh yourself. There's so much to tell you, so much," my mother said. "This man who came with you, who's he?"

"My servant, Salih," I explained.

My mother clapped her hands three times. A little serving girl appeared, her clothes clean, her hair neatly braided down her back. "Bulbul," my mother said in a voice so authoritative I thought for a moment that she'd been ordering servants about for twenty years, "see to it that this man is given water to wash with and something to eat. And bring sherbet and sweetmeats out here to the courtyard immediately." She turned to me and shook her head. "I don't know where we're going to put him," she said. "We don't have enough room for our own servants as it is. We're building more rooms, but the work goes so slowly."

"I have another one too," I admitted almost guiltily. "He's coming with the luggage. But don't worry about them. I'll put them up at a khan."

My mother didn't protest. I was glad to sit down then on one of the fine new carpets that filled the freshly paved courtyard. My head was whirling. "My sisters," I repeated, "where are they?"

"Married," my father said. "Thanks to our new position in this city, we were able to arrange matches for them with wonderful husbands, good men."

"And men of substance," my mother added with a sigh of satisfaction.

"Sharifah is next," my father said. "She'll be married within the month."

"I'm getting the best husband of all," Sharifah added complacently. "He's Idris, the son of Walid the physician."

"Well, that's wonderful to hear," I congratulated her. "I'm glad I won't miss your wedding, as I did the others."

"O my daughter," my father said, "forgive us for that. But we didn't know when you'd be back, or even if. The young men didn't want to wait."

"To tell you the truth," my mother added drily, "neither did Fatimah or Khalidah or Zaynab."

My father touched my hand. "Why didn't you send a message, some word, so we could know where you were, what you were doing, how you were feeling?"

"I sent you money," I said. "I thought that would make it clear to you that I was very, very well. But it was important that no one in Tyre guess my true identity. I could never have done what I did if they'd known there that I was a woman. Messages could have been dangerous."

My father nodded. "I guessed as much. But it doesn't matter anymore. Now everyone can know what marvelous things you've done. Such matters can't be kept secret. They'll be spoken of in every bathhouse in Baghdad, in every shop in the bazaar."

"Everyone probably knows already," my mother

interjected. "That porter you hired is the most energetic gossip in the city."

"He needs work," my father apologized, looking at me. "He has a dozen children."

"Father," I told him, "the money I sent you is yours. It's yours to do with as you please. You don't have to account to anyone for the way you spend it—least of all to me. I have more to give you—much more."

My mother stared at me. "That goes without saying. You're home now. All that you have is his."

I returned her look, holding her eyes with mine. "Of course. If I need more, I'll earn it."

My mother pressed her lips tightly together. When she opened them again, it was to say, "That's all over with. Now that you're home, you'll behave as befits a modest woman."

I stood up, walked over to her, knelt at her side. I took her hands in mine. "Mother, you can't erase the two and a half years I've lived through. You can't pretend they haven't happened. Nothing is the same, for you or for me."

My mother shook her hands free of mine and turned to my father. "How can you let her talk this way? It's against nature. It's against God."

But he didn't reply. He only smiled his melancholy smile.

And as the days passed, he deferred to me in everything. He made no purchase without asking my advice, embarked on no enterprise without discussing it with me first. As in the old days, we sat in the courtyard in the evenings, talking about business, but now it was he who asked the questions and I who answered them. And we played chess too, as in former times, only now we used a board and pieces made of teakwood inlaid with ivory that I'd bought for him in Damascus.

Once, while we played, my father said to me, "These chess pieces are magnificent, Buran. They're so magnificent I feel sometimes as if I should just look at them, not soil them by playing with them. If you still have the white queen I gave you the morning you left, we could play with the old set now and then."

"I don't have it," I said. "I gave it to a friend. But not just any friend," I added quickly. I didn't want him to think I had treated his talisman lightly. "I gave it to the best friend I ever had or ever will have."

"Who is she?" my father asked.

"She?" My smile was a bit rueful, I suppose. "It was a man, Father. His name isn't important. I'll never see him again. He doesn't know who I really am. After all, how could I tell him?"

At that time, my father didn't press me. Neither he nor my mother really wanted to think about the things that had happened to me during my time away from them. They wanted to pretend that the money we now all enjoyed was a mysterious gift from heaven. My mother would also have liked to pretend that I hadn't changed, that I was no different from any of my sisters, or at least not in any important way. That was harder to do. If I hadn't been there, she might have succeeded, but my actual presence made that impossible. I continued to conduct business. I did it through my father, but I was the one who told him what to do. My mother didn't like it very much, but she saw no way out of it. She had been poor too long not to fear poverty's return.

On one issue, though, my parents were in perfect agreement. And on one issue neither of them gave me any peace. The caravan merchant who had wanted me for his son called and was sent on his way again without much ceremony. But that didn't close the subject of my marrying. It came up every day. The conversation was always the same. Only the names changed.

"Abu Jamil came to see me today," my father would say.

"Abu Jamil? Abu Jamil?" my mother would query, pretending ignorance. "Is that the Abu Jamil who manages the caliph's business affairs?"

"None other," my father would reply.

"And is his son that Jamil we run into sometimes when we're shopping at the bazaar? What a marvelous looking fellow he is. How the girls sigh if they're lucky enough to cross his path. I think they purposely arrange to be at the stalls they think he's likely to visit when they suspect he might be there."

"The same," my father would assure her. "The very same."

"Well, then, my husband," my mother would recite dutifully, "what did the respected Abu Jamil want with you?"

"He wants our Buran for his son. His son, he says, is desperate with love. He'll die if he can't have her, poor fellow."

Now it was my turn. "Oh, nonsense, Father. He's never even seen me. How can he be desperate with love for me?"

"He's heard of you, Buran," my father would reply. "Everyone's heard of you. Such things as you've accomplished can't be kept secret. They're spoken of in every shop in Baghdad. Everyone knows you're rich and beautiful. Everyone wants to marry you."

"But I don't want to marry everyone, Father," I would snap. "I don't want to marry anyone."

"But you must," my mother would insist. "You must marry. We all must marry. You're a lucky girl. You have some say in the matter. Your father is too kind."

Then my father would raise his hand. "My wife, we agreed. She's the one who's doing the marrying. She's to choose."

"So choose *someone*," my mother would cry. "There must be one man in all of Baghdad who'll satisfy your highness."

"There isn't," I'd reply stubbornly. "Not in all of Baghdad."

"Not in all the world," my mother would shoot back.

To that I didn't reply. There was a man, one man, in all the world, who would satisfy me very well. If I couldn't have him, I'd take no one, let my father wheedle and my mother cry all they would. I loved them both very much. I obeyed them when I could. But the time was long past when I could give myself away to satisfy their notions of propriety.

But one day the conversation was different. Spring had come again. I sat poring over my accounts, while Salih fanned me. It wasn't really warm enough for that yet, but Salih liked to attend me and so I had to find things for him to do.

My father and mother came into the room together. It was my room, a large new room we'd added to the house since I'd come home. The place sprawled now like a rabbit warren, arched iwan after arched iwan leading into one courtyard after another, off which our new rooms opened. We'd had to buy the houses of Abu Rashid and Abu Tahir, at ridiculous prices, to make room for our growth. We could have moved ourselves, of course, but my father wouldn't hear of it. He'd been born in this house, he said, and he'd die in it. He'd moved the shop to larger quarters, and that was enough moving for him. "Besides," he added, somewhat mysteriously, "if someone comes looking for me, let him know where to find me."

"Listen to this, Buran," my father said. "Listen to this proposition."

My mother was smiling. "This one you'll attend to, my daughter," she said. "I'm sure of that."

I longed to tell them I never wanted to hear another word spoken on the subject of my marriage, but they were my parents and I couldn't say that. I lay down my quill pen, pushed away my accounts, and looked up at them with as much expectancy in my glance as I could manage.

"You'll never guess who came to see me today," my father said.

"I can't imagine," I replied, pretending interest.

"He used to call on me every day—before."

"Before you got rich?" Now I really was interested.

He nodded.

"But he calls on you no longer?"

Again he nodded.

"That could only be my uncle." Envy had put a stop to his brotherly concern.

"Yes," my father responded gleefully. "Your uncle." He sat down on the cushion next to mine. My mother sat down too. "He wants you to marry Hassan. Actually, he doesn't really care which of his sons you marry—any one of them would do. But he knows you fancy Hassan, and besides, Hassan is the eldest, so that's the one he offers."

"Aren't you pleased?" my mother cried. "Aren't you happy? You can have Hassan now. You always wanted him."

But wanted him no longer. "Ah, yes," I replied coolly. "But does Hassan want me?"

"Want you? Want you?" my father exclaimed. "He can scarcely restrain himself, he's so eager for the match."

"Times have changed, haven't they?" I remarked softly.

My mother either didn't catch or chose to ignore the irony in my voice. "Of course it's most suitable," she said. "The same blood runs in both your veins."

I smiled. I exulted. I couldn't help it. But I managed to swallow my laughter. "Most suitable," I agreed. "If I must marry, then I must marry. Let it be to my cousin, rather than to a total stranger. Tell my uncle I will have Hassan."

"Allah be praised," my mother sighed.

"On one condition," I added quickly. "On one condition only."

"Condition?" my mother queried sharply. "Condition? What condition?"

I turned to my father. "I won't marry a man who bears a tattoo."

"What kind of nonsense is that?" my mother exclaimed. "Why would Hassan have someone's mark on him? He's not a slave."

"Oh, I daresay his body is clean of any such disfigurement," I replied casually. "It's just a silly notion I have. I'm afraid of marrying a man who belongs to someone else. If he'll submit his body to your inspection, Father, and it bears no marks, I'll marry him."

"You're crazy, Buran," my mother said. Her voice carried profound conviction. It wasn't the first time she'd made such a statement.

"Marks like that disgust me," I explained apologetically. "I know it may sound absurd to you, but I'm in a position not to have to marry a man who disgusts me."

My mother snorted. My father said merely, "I'll attend to it. You're the one who's doing the marrying." He left immediately to call upon my uncle and explain the condition. He didn't want to waste any time. Perhaps he was afraid I'd change my mind.

The evening dragged by slowly. My mother and I both managed to keep ourselves busy, but my mind was not on my accounts; her mind was not on her spinning. We were both imagining the scene taking place at my uncle's house; but though we didn't compare our versions, I knew as surely as I loved Mahmud that the picture in my mind was very different from the one in hers.

When my father came home, it was apparent from his face that two emotions were warring in him at once. All the color had left his cheeks and his skin was nearly as gray as his beard. At the same time he was struggling not to smile. Something had happened to shock him, but the very same event amused him too.

As he entered my room, my mother followed behind him. She didn't wait for him to sit down. "Well?" she asked. "What happened? Tell us. Tell us this instant."

"I will," my father replied calmly. "Just give me a chance." He arranged himself comfortably on some of the pillows scattered around the carpet. He did this very slowly. My mother almost exploded with impatience, but she kept quiet. She knew my father. If she pushed him too far, he would move even more slowly, if that were possible, and an even longer time would pass before she heard what she wanted to hear.

"Sit down too, O my mother," I invited. She threw me an irritated glance, but she followed my suggestion. At last my father was ready.

"Your uncle, like your mother, thinks you're crazy," my father began.

"How dare he!" my mother interrupted. She might criticize her children or even her husband, but from the aspersions of anyone else, strangers or kin, she'd defend us with the fury of a tiger.

"If you want to know what happened," my father said pleasantly, "try listening."

My mother flushed, and held her peace.

"I'll tell you the whole story," my father went on, "and I'll tell it in my own way. It's a good story." My mother nodded. I nodded. He rubbed his hands together and nodded, too. "I told your uncle your condition, Buran. That's when he said that you were crazy. He added a few other choice remarks, such as 'How can you permit her to behave so outrageously?' I didn't even answer that one. He knows the situation as well as I do. I just said, 'She's the one doing the marrying. If Hassan wants her, he'll have to submit.' So your uncle sent for Hassan."

"Naturally," my mother said.

I didn't say anything. I knew what was coming next.

"Hassan came into the room," my father continued. "Your uncle said to him, 'Hassan, your cousin Buran is crazy. She demands a test of your good faith. But she's very rich and very beautiful, and her fortune shouldn't go out of the family. So submit to her little test. It doesn't mean anything.'

" 'Well,' Hassan said, 'what's the test?'

" 'Explain it to him,' your uncle said.

" 'Well,' I said, 'Buran merely wants me to inspect your person. She wants to make sure you carry no mark that would signify your allegiance to someone else, no blemish to mar your physical perfection. As your father says, it's nothing.'

"But Hassan blanched white as cotton. 'That's demeaning,' he cried. He was furious. 'I'll submit to no such inspection. I'm not a slave.' His father begged and pleaded with both of us. He begged me to rescind the demand. But all I said was that it was your demand, and since you were the one doing the marrying, you had the right to ask what you would. He begged Hassan to give in. But Hassan was adamant. He absolutely refused. 'You'd have to kill me first,' he said." My father shrugged and spread out his hands, glee and disappointment warring in his face. "I made inquiries on my way home at the public bath nearest my brother's house. Hassan hasn't been in there since he returned from Alexandria." My father lifted his eyebrows. "I think you know something, Buran; something that we don't."

I smiled a little, but I didn't say a word. It was not for me to betray my cousin's secret.

"We're ruined," my mother sighed. "She loves Hassan. If she can't marry him, she'll have no one. But I can't say that I blame her. Who would want to marry a man with someone's mark on his body?"

"Poor Hassan," I said. "How far he's fallen."

"Well," my father said, "it isn't over yet. Your uncle has offered Ali. It seems," he added drily, "that Ali is as desperate in his love for you today as Hassan was yesterday."

"Ali?" My mother snorted. "If she can't have Hassan, what makes your brother think she'll marry a weasel like Ali?"

My tone was resigned. "If I must marry, then I must marry. It might as well be my cousin rather than a total stranger. Tell my uncle I'll marry Ali—but he must submit to the same test I demanded of Hassan."

My mother and my father both looked at me, and then, as if they were both puppets worked by the same hand, they nodded. My father carried my message back to my uncle the very next day. Of course, the results were the same. Ali, like Hassan before him, refused to submit to my father's inspection of his person. My father reported that my uncle's fury was horrible to behold. But Ali would not be moved. His rejection of the idea was absolute.

So then my uncle offered Ibrahim, and then Sulayman, and then Antar. He even offered Ismael and Gamal, who were much younger than I. To poor little Gamal, his last hope, my uncle even took the whip. But it didn't matter. Gamal was no more to be persuaded to submit to my father's inspection than were any of his brothers. He told his own father why, and he told him why in my father's hearing. It was no great trick for my father and my uncle to figure out that Gamal's brothers, if their tongues had been as loosely hinged, or if the whip had been laid across their backs, would have told the same story. Perhaps at some point my uncle actually did get it out of them. But my father didn't have to hear it over and over again. Once was enough.

In despair, my uncle at last gave up. He had to admit that there would be no wedding between one of his sons and me. "My sons aren't good enough for your daughter," he admitted.

"Don't be too upset," my father reported comforting his brother. "The money won't go out of the family. Buran won't marry any of your sons, but if I know my daughter, she probably won't marry anyone else either."

"And what did he say when you said that?" I asked. "Was he comforted?"

"No, as a matter of fact," my father said, grinning. "He was more upset than ever. He knows perfectly well that if you die unmarried, your fortune will pass to your sisters' children."

"Yes," my mother agreed wryly. "To your sisters' children. So far as your uncle's concerned, that's out of the family. By family he means only *his* family. He can't understand that your father isn't exactly dismayed at the thought of your money, as well as his own, descending eventually to his own grandchildren."

Even she had to smile at that thought. It was as if it were a new one that had just occurred to her. After that she stopped pressing me to marry.

My father stopped pressing, too. He wouldn't have been human if he hadn't taken a certain pleasure in my uncle's discomfort, though he'd never have admitted it out loud, not even to me. Occasionally though, in the weeks that followed, he said things like, "Oh, Buran, when your mother and I are gone, what will you do? Your life will be so lonely." That's how I knew that although, like my mother, he was at last convinced I'd die unwed, the prospect certainly didn't please him.

"Don't worry about me," I told him one day. "I'll

take a couple of my sisters' children to live with me. They'll have so many, they won't miss one or two."

His face flushed with anger. "O my daughter," he scolded, "what a foolish thing to say. Do you think because I had six children at home, I didn't long for you when you were gone? You know a lot, my daughter, but there are some things you don't know at all. You have no heart."

"I have a heart, Father."

"Then where is it?"

"Far away," I answered softly. "Far away with someone I can never have." I turned away then so he couldn't see the tears that had sprung to my eyes.

"Why not?" he asked sharply. "It seems to me you could have whomever you wanted."

"He doesn't know who I am," I replied. "He doesn't know where I am."

"He's the one who has the white queen," my father guessed.

I looked at him again and nodded silently.

"I suspected as much. If he found out where you are, he'd come."

"I don't think so. I wasn't honest with him. He must hate me—if he thinks about me at all."

"He doesn't hate you," my father said. "He may be annoyed with you—that's not hard. But hate you—never."

"Well," I replied with an attempt at lightness, "it doesn't matter. He'll never come to me. I'm not going to tell him where I am, and there's no other way for him to find out."

"Do you want him to find you?" my father asked, his voice low and serious.

The truth now, I told myself, the truth. He was asking for the truth, and I could do no less than give it to him. But when I looked into my soul, I realized that I didn't know the truth. I didn't know whether I wanted Mahmud to find me or not. "I long for him with all my being," I said at last. "But if he knew the truth about me, he wouldn't come. He would have to despise me for the lie that's between us."

My father didn't ask me any more questions about Mahmud. I had thought I was done crying for him, but now the pain of his loss returned with all the sharpness of a fresh wound. At night, when I was alone in my bed, I took to weeping. I wept as I hadn't wept since that long-ago day I had sailed away from Tyre, knowing that each gust of wind blew me farther and farther away from my heart's true friend. I wept for all the lonely years that stretched in front of me like an empty track through the desert. Of what use was it to be rich as the caliph if there was to be no one in the world that loved me best, no one in the world whom I loved best? The revenge I'd achieved on Hassan was as empty as death. I'd have given it over in an instant for five minutes with Mahmud. What good is revenge when you're alone at night?

But with morning, and all that I had to do, I

managed to push Mahmud and my loneliness, if not quite out of my mind, at least to the bottom of it, where it belonged. When I was wide awake and in control, I knew better than to weep over what I couldn't do anything about. It was only in the echoing dark that I couldn't help myself. It was then I realized that the pain of my loneliness would not, as I had thought, grow less with time. Even if the image of Mahmud himself might fade with the passing of years, the loneliness would just feel worse as its accumulation crushed me.

But loneliness was better than marriage to some fortune-hunter, some insensitive lout or condescending aristocrat. Even though my parents no longer pressed me, suitors still abounded. Every day Muhsin and Salih, with the help of my father's porter, turned another one away from the door. Or if he was too important to come himself, they turned away his friend, or servant, or hired matchmaker, or whomever it was he chose to send. Occasionally, one of them offered a bribe sufficient to subvert even Salih and Muhsin. Those who managed to get through the outer defenses, my father was forced to see; and if I sought a brief moment of amusement, I saw them myself, behind heavy veils. Sometimes I wondered if I might find one who would tell me the truth. If one of them had said that he wanted to marry me for the help I could give him in business, I might have been tempted. It would have been like a trading partnership. Perhaps

I could have borne that, and it would have been good to have a child. But all I ever heard were hymns to my beauty or protestations of undying love from swains who'd never laid eyes on my face or heard more than two words issue from my lips. I could only laugh.

About six or eight weeks after I had told my father that I loved a man, a particularly persistent suitor bribed his way past Salih and Muhsin. My father was at the shop, and when they told me the suitor was from Orontes, I agreed to meet him. I veiled my face and received him in the second courtyard, keeping both Salih and Muhsin beside me.

He bowed as he stood before me. "Peace be with you, honored lady," he said in a deep, pleasant voice. He was no longer young, but he was tall and straight, with ruddy skin, sharp blue eyes, and a thick, dark beard streaked with gray. "I have traveled far to bring you greetings today."

"To you, peace," I returned. "Please, make yourself comfortable." I gestured toward the rug opposite the one on which I was seated. "Salih, fetch some yogurt."

Salih entered the house quietly. "I'm honored that you have received me," the man said. "I understand it isn't your usual custom."

"Well," I replied, "you've come from far away. It seemed the least I could do. I didn't think your journey should be entirely in vain."

"It won't be in vain," he replied confidently. "You'll return with me to Orontes as my bride."

I was tempted to snort, but I restrained myself. "Why should I?" I asked.

"Because I love you," he replied. "And I'll teach you to love me." He smiled suggestively and shrugged his shoulders lightly. He was telling me that women found his blue eyes irresistible.

I sighed. When he had first walked into the court-yard, so upright and handsome, and clearly no mere boy, I'd hoped that he would be the one to have something different to say. I should have known better. Still, I wasn't ready to send him away. I was curious. I had been courted by countless suitors from Baghdad, and from Aleppo, and from Damascus, but this was the first to come to me from so far away as Orontes. "Are you in Baghdad simply to call on me, or did other business bring you here?"

"To call on you only, fair lady," he replied. "Why else? For a native of Orontes, Baghdad holds no wonders. But you'll see that for yourself when you get there."

"How did you hear of me, all the way in Orontes?" I asked.

My question seemed to surprise him. "But lady, surely you know that you're famous. Your story is told in bazaars and khans in every city from the Persian Gulf to the sea."

Now I was surprised. "Surely not," I demurred.

"I speak the truth," the man said. "Your servant goes to the bazaar. He talks to men who've crossed the desert with caravans. He'll tell you that what I say is true."

I turned toward Muhsin. He nodded. "Lady, our brother from Orontes is right. You're famous everywhere. Such things as you have done cannot be kept secret."

"What do they say of me?" My face warmed with a rush of blood, and I was grateful for the veil that covered my embarrassment.

The man from Orontes answered. "They tell the whole story—how you acquired a fortune in business and then came back to this city to revenge yourself on the cousins who had insulted you in the days when you were poor. They say too that you're as beautiful as you're clever. Naturally," he added complacently, "when I heard the tale I came as quickly as I could. If I heard it in Orontes, they've heard it in all the other ports, too. You'd be best off marrying me immediately. Otherwise you'll be so besieged with suitors, you'll go out of your mind. It'll be more than you and your poor father can handle."

"I've been besieged already," I informed him firmly. "We've handled it so far. I daresay we can continue to manage." I rose from my seat. "I thank you for the honor you've done me," I said, "but I have no desire to marry you, no desire whatsoever. You may go now."

He remained where he was. "I must speak with your father first," he said. "It's for him to dismiss me, not you."

I shook my head. In spite of all that he'd heard, he still didn't understand. Salih came into the court then, carrying a tray. "Our visitor will not be taking refreshment after all," I said. "Please, Salih, Muhsin, see him to the gate, and then return here. I want to talk to you."

"I told you," the man from Orontes began loudly, "I told you I'm not ready to . . ." But he never finished his sentence. Salih grabbed one of his forearms and Muhsin the other. They lifted him to his feet, and before he realized what was happening to him, he was pressed through the iwan and out of my sight. He was through the gate nearly as quickly, for I had barely time to throw the stifling veils off my face before Salih and Muhsin were back in the courtyard.

I confronted them immediately. "You've gossiped about me," I accused. "You've sat in khans with travelers and told them all my story. Who gave you leave to talk about me as if I were a public spectacle?"

Immediately they both fell to their knees, their arms stretched out in front of them, their foreheads touching the ground. "Oh, stop it," I cried, losing patience. "Don't grovel. Just tell me the truth!"

Salih remained prone before me. Muhsin sat up on his haunches and spoke for both of them. "We wouldn't lie to you, lady," he said. "We never have, and we won't start now. If we take a bribe, it's only because it's so large that it's irresistible to poor men like us. Forgive us for that, lady."

"Have I ever mentioned it?" I asked. "I understand. What would have been the point of your leaving Tyre with me if not for an opportunity to make your fortune? But what has that to do with telling stories about me to strangers?"

"I wasn't the first to speak," Muhsin said, his face serious, his eyes looking directly into mine. "I swear by my father's head I wasn't the first. And neither was Salih."

"I swear by my father's head," Salih echoed, his voice muffled by the pavement.

"But," Muhsin added, "how could such a story as yours be kept secret?"

I began pacing up and down the courtyard, speaking as much to myself as to Muhsin. "The fact that I'm rich . . . of course I understand all Baghdad would know that. The way we live makes it no secret. But the marks my cousins bear? The way they acquired them? How did that come to be learned? *They* would never speak of it, that's certain. Their servants wouldn't either, because a master's disgrace always reflects on those in his employ. Isn't that true, Muhsin?" I asked, pausing before him.

"Yes, lady, it's true as the sun."

"Then, Muhsin," I continued sternly, my hand gripping his shoulder, "it must have been the servants in this house who spread the tale. And they must have spoken of it not only to citizens of Baghdad, but to traveling merchants, and to strangers. That wasn't right. I never meant for my cousins' shame to be known to the entire world. It was always enough for me that I knew of it, and that my parents and my uncle knew of it—quite enough."

Muhsin sighed. "Lady," he said, "if the servants in this house speak of the matter, it's because the chief of this house spoke of the matter. When he told the story, it seemed to the servants it was meant to be spoken of."

"My father? My father?" It was a thought that had never occurred to me. Although I knew my uncle had tormented him over the years, I'd always thought that my gentle father was cut from a different cloth than the rest of us. And though I knew he took a certain inevitable pleasure in the fact that his family had bested his brother's, I knew the pleasure was mixed with regret at my single state. I couldn't picture his gossiping about my uncle's and my cousins' discomfort.

But Muhsin loved my father almost as much as he loved me. He wouldn't say anything about him that wasn't true. "All right, Muhsin, Salih," I continued quietly, "I accept your explanation. I forgive you." Later I would get to the bottom of the matter. I turned toward the house. "I'll rest in my room for a while. Go now and watch at the gate. When my father comes home, tell me."

I went to see him as soon as I heard that he was in the house. He sat in the courtyard telling his beads, as he usually did while he waited for supper. I was very angry. He could see it in my face. "Why, daughter," he said in his usual calm, easy tone, "what's happened to you? Your face looks like a stormcloud."

"A suitor came to me today," I said.

"You shouldn't receive them. That's my task."

"It's not the suitors," I returned impatiently. "I'm over being angry at them."

"That's something," he replied mildly.

"It was where he was from. He was from Orontes."

"Orontes?" His forehead wrinkled. "What do you have against Orontes? You've never even been there. Neither have I, of course, but I've heard it's a beautiful city, and so far away—farther than any city you have visited."

"That's the point, Father. How did a man from Orontes come to hear of me?" My voice was as accusing as a judge's. "Not only of me, but of all my cousins too, and their disgrace? How, Father, did I come to be the subject of common gossip—world wide common gossip, if such a thing can be imagined!"

My father didn't appear disturbed. "Not gossip, daughter," he said, "unless the stories Shahrazad told are gossip. Perhaps if we'd known the people those stories are about, we'd call them gossip too. Your story is a tale like those, passed from one teller to another. How could such things as you have done be kept secret?"

"I told no one," I retorted. "You can be sure my uncle and my cousins didn't. I thought you were above such pettiness. I'm disappointed."

My father snorted. "What makes you think I'm any better than you are? I'm not, that's certain. But I didn't tell your story to make my nephews, and you, the subject of idle gossip. I told it for a reason. I hear you, sometimes, weeping in the night. And I see your eyes, sometimes, staring into the distance, and I know you're far away from us, in another place. I'm a father. Am I to hear and see such things and do nothing about them?"

As usual, his calm, affectionate voice dissipated my temper. It wasn't easy to be angry at my father. Even my mother had always had difficulty maintaining righteous indignation before his quiet reasonableness. I took his hand. "But Father," I said softly, "I don't understand how telling the whole tale to strangers from caravans who come into the shop will do me or anyone else any good at all."

"Oh, good will come of it, my daughter, wait and see." His hand squeezed mine. "You may know all there is to know about making money, but I've lived longer than you, and I know a lot more than you about the mysteries of the human heart. Good will come from it. Mark my words." Then he laughed loudly, joyfully, without even a tinge of melancholy. "Besides, my daughter, how could such a thing be kept secret? Tell me that. How could such a thing be kept secret?"

I didn't answer. I had no answer. He was right, of course. Just as Baghdad had learned of my wealth, and the fact that I'd earned it myself, so the city was bound sooner or later to know the story of me and my cousins. And if Baghdad knew the story, the rest of the world would know it too, in one way or another, in one shape or another. But why had my father himself been the one to first tell the tale? He said good would come of it. I didn't understand what he meant by that, not then.

And though I asked him every night, every night, "What good has come of it yet? What good is it that you expect?" he never really answered me.

He only laughed and repeated, "O my daughter, how could such a thing be kept secret? Tell me that. How could such a thing be kept secret?"

And though I didn't understand what he meant by good coming, I believed him. I was as wakeful at night as I had ever been. But I didn't weep anymore. Instead I lay on my bed, waiting, waiting. I didn't know what I was waiting for, but I knew that I was waiting. At times my whole body tingled with anticipation. Something was going to happen.

Only it didn't happen. Days went by, weeks, a month, and nothing happened. Well, that's not true. Things happened. Things happened every day. But the thing, whatever it was, for which my heart was waiting —that did not happen.

And then it was Aminah's wedding. The festivals and ceremonies went on for a week. The final entertainment was even more magnificent than the one my parents had made for Sharifah. With great rejoicing we ate, we drank, we sang, we danced all over our sprawling house. And then, amid laughter and celebration, all the guests led Aminah through the streets to the house her bridegroom had built for her on the Karkh, the other side of the river. After more feasting and revelry, we came home again. The guests drifted away, leaving our courtyards full of soiled plates and half-empty cups. The servants were too weary to clean up that night. It would all have to wait until morning.

It had been the longest day of my life. I had awakened at dawn to make sure the feast was properly prepared. I had helped Aminah dress and make up. I had greeted the guests—and served many of them with my own hands. But now, so many hours later, though my legs ached and my arms drooped, I knew that I wouldn't be able to sleep. My father, my mother, and Darirah went to bed. My other sisters had long since departed with their husbands and their babies. I sat in the courtyard outside of my room, staring up at the stars. Usually, when I gazed at them, I remembered the desert and was filled with peace. It was different that night. I couldn't stop thinking.

Aminah had a husband. Soon it would be Darirah's turn. My father and mother, in the course of time, would die. Then I would be alone. It was what I had chosen. I didn't want the marriages my sisters had. It was better to be alone. But it would have been best to have been with Mahmud.

A wave of regret washed over me. My heart constricted in my chest, and I felt as if I were drowning. My mind couldn't believe what was happening to me. How could I succumb to an emotion as useless as regret?

But my poor heart ignored my mind's scolding. It went right on aching. Tears coursed down my face, like two rivers in spring.

Somehow, the tears helped. The knife stopped turning inside of me. The agony was replaced by a sweeter pain. I could breathe again.

I rose and walked across the courtyard, through the arched iwan, across another court, and out through the gate into the street. No modest woman, no matter how heavily she had veiled her face, ever ventured into the street alone after dark. But I didn't care. It was so late that even immodest women were no longer abroad—only Buran, sometimes called Nasir, who this night didn't know who she was.

I traversed the route I had journeyed twice before

in my life—once when I had left Baghdad and once when I had returned. The streets were silent except for the occasional yowling of a dog, and, further on, the quiet lapping of the river against its banks. I walked briskly, and I was glad of the exercise. I had missed it, all these months since I had come home.

I crossed the bridge and strode on, following the river until I had left the city behind me and was walking now in open country, where the irrigated plain met the desert's edge. The air was cool and dry and I breathed it deeply, swinging my arms as I moved. I knew I should turn and go back. Dawn was only an hour or two away. I ought to be home again before anyone in the household woke and missed me.

But I wasn't worried about getting lost. The moon was still bright. If I kept in my sight the line of growth that marked the river, I couldn't get lost. And it was so good to be out-of-doors, so good to be walking freely. If only I could ride again. If only there were some way I could keep a horse. If I put my mind to it, perhaps I would find a way. . . .

Moonlight faded, and the first faint streaks of morning lit the horizon. My mind was on the problem of a horse; it was difficult, in the dim light, to make out even an acacia tree unless it was no more than ten paces in front of my nose. I didn't even see the string of camels until they were almost upon me. It was a small string, half a dozen. Three of the beasts carried goods on their backs; the other three carried men.

A spasm of fear seized my stomach. What was this small caravan doing out in the desert before dawn? Either it had been traveling all night, or else it had packed up and moved out of its camp well before dawn. Neither action was the normal behavior of respectable merchants. What was their errand, that they would creep silently across rock and sand in the near darkness?

But they must have been equally amazed at the sight of me, a woman, alone, walking in what was still the night. The camels halted. The man in the lead called out to me. "Peace be with you, traveler. In the name of the Prophet, is all well with you?"

I recognized the voice. As soon as the first sounds had issued from his mouth, I knew the name of the man riding the lead camel. Tears sprang to my eyes. I was turning into a fountain. But these were such different tears from the ones I had shed a few hours before.

"And to you, peace," I responded. I called out loudly, even though I couldn't keep my voice from trembling. "All is very well with me. All is very well *now*, my prince."

All three of the camels bearing men knelt instantly, as if in response to a common signal. The man in the lead was off his mount's back before the others had even removed their feet from the stirrups. He seemed to leap across the rocky patch of ground that separated us.

Then I cried out. "Mahmud!"

He pulled me to him. His arms went around me, hard and strong, squeezing the breath from my body so that I couldn't speak another word. I didn't want to speak another word. I clung to him as if I were drowning, as hungry for his presence as a starving man is for food. Alone in the desert, in the strange half-light that precedes the dawn, we dared to embrace.

But after a few moments I pulled myself away. Now the sky was streaked with pink. I wanted to look at him. Was he the same Mahmud? No, not the same, anymore than I was the same. He was thinner and harder, and there were little lines around his eyes. But he was Mahmud, nevertheless, Mahmud, my prince.

"You have forgiven me," I said. It was a statement, not a question.

His arms were still around me, and they pressed me close to him again. "Forgiven you?" he asked, smiling a little. "My heart, you still talk in riddles. What do I have to forgive you for?"

"Deceiving you," I whispered.

"You did what you had to do to save your family, to save yourself," he replied, his voice gruff. "I deceived myself, and because of that I almost lost you. When I think of the months. . . . O my heart. . . ." His voice choked; he could say no more. As if from a great distance, I heard houdajs creak and tails flick. Afterwards, for a long time, I heard nothing but the beating of my own heart and Mahmud's. Minutes passed, many, many minutes, before we spoke again.

But we couldn't embrace forever, not even the two of us, who had waited so long to share our embraces. Sunrise is rapid in the desert and full morning light struck my eyes. "Mahmud, I must return to my house," I said.

"Indeed you must," he replied softly. His fingers reached up and pulled a strand of hair away from my face. "I think you had better make yourself presentable first. You parents mustn't think ill of me before I've had a chance to explain."

We washed our faces in the river, and I straightened my hair and my clothes as best I could. Mahmud called out to Faris. He led the camels toward us. I mounted one, Mahmud another, and the guide rode the third. Faris walked in front of the three beasts that carried supplies, leading them with a rope.

I was full of questions, and so, no doubt, was Mahmud, but we didn't talk much as we rode toward the city. It was enough to be together. We had years and years in which to tell each other stories.

When we reached our courtyard, I sent the porter to wake my parents. They came to meet us side by side, their eyes still full of sleep.

"Peace be with you," Mahmud called out as soon as he saw them. He didn't want to waste a moment. He didn't want to give them time to misunderstand. "I am Mahmud, son of the Wali of Tyre."

"And to you, peace," my father replied. "Your presence does honor to my humble house." But he didn't sound or look the least bit surprised. He behaved like a man receiving a guest he'd been expecting for a long time.

"My unceremonious arrival at such an unconscionable hour surely requires an explanation," Mahmud began in the formal, faintly pompous manner which, I was amused to realize, he still adopted when he found himself in a slightly uncomfortable situation. "Especially," he added, "as I come, unexpectedly, in the company of your daughter."

"I know your explanations," my father replied bluntly. "You love her. You wish to marry her. My only question is, why did it take you so long to get here?"

My father may not have been surprised at Mahmud, but Mahmud was surprised at my father. "She told you about me," he blurted out.

"Not in words," my father smiled. "I didn't know your name. But I know enough so that now I can wait for your story. Come, my son. Rest. Eat. Then we'll talk."

A sigh escaped Mahmud's lips. He relaxed and obeyed. Later, we sat in the shaded inner court, eating bread, fruit, and cheese, while Mahmud told us how he had found me. We were all there, my mother, my father, Darirah, and me. Already it was as if Mahmud were a member of the family.

"I followed Nas . . . Buran to Alexandria," my prince explained, "but it was too late." He turned to me as he spoke. "I docked just a few hours after you had sailed. I was disappointed, but I didn't despair. In Alexandria they knew of a wealthy woman traveling alone except for her two servants. You had done a lot of business in the city before you left; you'd made your mark. Along the wharves, it wasn't hard to discover that you'd gone to Cyprus. But the journey to Cyprus was another matter. We were becalmed, and then we sprang a leak. We had to put in for repairs. A five-day journey took us three weeks." His face, his voice grew bleak with remembered anguish. As he told the story, he was reliving the hope and the frustration that had racked him alternately, or even at the same moment, during the months he had sought me. My heart ached for what he had suffered, even though it was over now. I had had my work and my family to occupy me, and still I had felt a misery so deep it had kept me awake during the long, dark hours of the night. How much worse it must have been for him, who had no distractions, whose mind was occupied with only one concern—the goal of his quest—me. But my heart was full of joy too. It's a wonderful thing to know someone loves you best.

No one interrupted Mahmud. My father leaned forward, eager to catch every word. Darirah's eyes were round with wonder, and she didn't take them off Mahmud's face for a moment. My mother's hands for once were idle, her spindle lying in her lap. "In Cyprus I lost your trail completely." Mahmud's voice was low and full of sorrow. "You didn't stay there long, I suppose, and by the time I got there, you were only half-remembered. Other travelers had come through, perhaps even another woman accompanied by servants. The people I spoke to were confused. Some of them seemed to recall someone resembling my description of you, but they told conflicting stories about where she had gone after she had left Cyprus. One said Sidon, another said Yafa. I chose Yafa; Sidon was too close to Tyre, I thought." He shook his head emphatically. "A waste of time. No one in Yafa had heard of a woman merchant traveling with two servants. So then I went to Sidon. Your trail was cold. You'd been there weeks ago, some said, but no one knew where you'd gone. I wandered aimlessly from city to city. Sometimes I heard of a wealthy woman, a woman who did business. No one ever knew her name. No one ever knew where she was from They had ideas about where she had gone, but no one was ever sure. Sometimes I heard she was old and traveling entirely alone. Sometimes I heard she was young and traveling with a huge retinue. Whatever I heard, it was never quite right. It was never quite you. But it was enough to keep me going, to keep me looking. At last I came to Iconuim."

"Iconuim!" my mother cried, amazed. "Iconuim, so far away."

"Yes, so far away," Mahmud agreed. "And there,

in a caravansary, I sat with a merchant. I made a habit of striking up friendships with merchants or sailors or caravan chiefs. They know more than other people." I thought of Gindar and Abu Sinan and Jihha. With their knowledge they had changed my life.

"And this merchant told me a strange tale." Now Mahmud's voice took on the intonation of a story-teller entertaining a crowd in the bazaar. "He laughed as he told it to me. He had heard it, he said, in Antioch. It was about a woman, a woman as clever as Princess Shahrazad. All by herself she had made a fortune in trade, and then she had returned home to achieve a marvelously appropriate revenge on cousins who had insulted her when she was poor. 'What a woman!' he cried when he was done with his story. 'If the three wives I already have weren't just about as much as I can manage, I'd seek her hand myself.'"

For the first time since he'd begun his tale, Mahmud smiled. "While I listened to him, my heart was so full of exultation I could hardly keep from shouting. He thought he was entertaining me with a story, as Shahrazad entertained the Sultan Shariah. But I knew immediately that he was talking about a real person. I knew immediately that the woman he spoke of could be no other than my beloved. 'Listen,' I said to that merchant, 'you couldn't have her even if you sought her. She's already promised.'" Mahmud paused and turned his full gaze upon me. "It may have been fool-ish of me," he said quietly, "but I knew, I knew from all that had passed between us, and from the white queen that you had left behind for me, I knew that you loved me. I was confident enough to believe that loving me, you wouldn't take another man, not if you could avoid it. And if there was a woman in the world who could avoid it, that woman was you!"

I wore no veil. After all that had passed between us, to what purpose would I have hidden my face from him? Even my mother couldn't insist upon it, though she and Darirah had covered theirs. So I didn't have to answer him. The smile I gave him was enough.

Mahmud returned to his story. "I asked the man if his informant had mentioned the name of this woman or her father's name. Those things he couldn't tell me. But he said the woman was one of seven daughters, and the cousins she had tricked were seven sons, and they all of them were said to live in Baghdad. And so I came here. I came here like the wind." Once more he addressed himself directly to me. "We were too close to the city last night for me to sleep. That's why you found me in the desert long before dawn. Something told you I was coming. That's why you were there too."

"O Mahmud!" I exclaimed. "Can the son of the Wali of Tyre marry a woman whose name is tossed around in bazaars and khans?"

"But Buran," Mahmud replied, his eyes, his mouth, his whole face smiling, "if your story hadn't been known, my hair could have been white before I found you. I would have, sooner or later. That I know. My wanderings would eventually have brought me to Baghdad. After I'd exhausted every port, I would have begun journeying inland, and sooner or later I would have come here. But that might not have been for years. It's because of the story that I found you as quickly as I did." His hand reached out and grasped mine. "Besides, how could such a thing be kept secret? Tell me that. How could such a thing be kept secret?"

My father's words rang out full and clear across the courtyard. "That's right, O son-in-law," he said. "How could such a thing be kept secret?"

A F T E R W O R D

AND SO IT WAS that Buran, *daughter of the poor shopkeeper known as Abu al-Banat, became the bride of Mahmud, prince of Tyre. For many years they ruled the city together. So great was their wisdom and understanding that under their joint stewardship, the city prospered beyond anything it had ever known before, or has been privileged to experience since. And when they grew old, Buran and Mahmud made sure that their children knew the strange and wonderful story of how they had come together, "because," Buran said, "children should not think that the blessings of Allah are theirs by right or come to them simply for the asking."*

Buran and Mahmud lived to celebrate the weddings of their grandchildren. They died within hours of each other; and when they were laid to rest, tears were shed for them not only in

Tyre, not only in Baghdad, but in all the lands caliph and sultan ruled.

One extraordinarily ancient and enormously fat man followed their funeral procession to the edge of the grave. Standing there, he was overheard to murmur to himself. "The ways of Allah are beyond human understanding," he said. "The father of sons lived to rue the day that they were born, and the father of daughters lived to become the companion of counselors and kings."

Seven Daughters and Seven Sons is a novel based on a folktale
that has been part of the oral tradition of Iraq since
the eleventh century of the common era.